BC-1   2010-11

CROSSING
the
TRACKS

CROSSING

the

TRACKS

BARBARA STUBER

Margaret K. McElderry Books
New York London Toronto Sydney

MARGARET K. McELDERRY BOOKS

An imprint of Simon & Schuster Children's Publishing Division

1230 Avenue of the Americas, New York, New York 10020

MARGARET K. McELDERRY BOOKS is a trademark of Simon & Schuster, Inc.

For information about special discounts for bulk purchases, please contact Simon & Schuster Special Sales at 1-866-506-1949 or business@simonandschuster.com.

The Simon & Schuster Speakers Bureau can bring authors to your live event. For more information or to book an event, contact the Simon & Schuster Speakers Bureau at 1-866-248-3049 or visit our website at www.simonspeakers.com.

Book design by Mike Rosamilia

The text for this book is set in MrsEaves.

Manufactured in the United States of America

10 9 8 7 6 5 4 3

Library of Congress Cataloging-in-Publication Data

Stuber, Barbara.

Crossing the tracks / Barbara Stuber.

p. cm.

Summary: In Missouri in 1926, fifteen-year-old Iris Baldwin discovers what family truly means when her father hires her out for the summer as a companion to a country doctor's invalid mother.

ISBN 978-1-4169-9703-0 (hardcover)

ISBN 978-1-4169-9705-4 (eBook)

[1. Families—Fiction. 2. Household employees—Fiction. 3. Missouri—History—20th century—Fiction.] I. Title.

PZ7.S937555Cr 2010

[Fic]—dc22   2009042672

To my grandmother
Ina May Baldwin Kohler

ACKNOWLEDGMENTS

My gratitude to the folks who inspired this story—the family members who have passed on and the characters I "met" through the magic of writing.

For excellent guidance and immense encouragement, I thank Judy Hyde, and also Laura Manivong, Elizabeth Bunce, Sue Gallion, Anola Pickett, Judy Schuler, Tessa Elwood, Victoria Dixon, and all the talented members of Heartland Writers for Kids and Teens.

Huge thanks to my kids—Anna for knowing Iris better than I do, Andy for his keen ear and good cheer when asked to listen to just one more chapter, and Austin for his incredible insight and humor.

Special thanks to my sister, Anne, for remembering and for having so much faith in me.

I am so very grateful to Ginger Knowlton for finding Iris the right home at Simon & Schuster, and to my editor, Karen Wojtyla, and to Emily Fabre, who so wisely walked Iris across the tracks.

Thanks to my dear friends for the power of their optimism and enthusiasm.

And, most importantly, love and gratitude to my husband, Jack, for the unwavering support, terrific ideas, patience, and loving kindness he has shown me from the very first moment I decided I wanted to write.

PROLOGUE

ATCHISON, KANSAS—NOVEMBER 1916

I'm under Mama's coffin. My little house in the center of the parlor has silky black curtain walls and a hard ceiling that I can touch with the top of my head if I sit cross-legged and stretch my neck. They moved all the furniture against the walls except a little round stool right by the coffin box, so even short people can see Mama this afternoon. That's why I'm wearing my scratchy church dress with the purple bows.

"Iris!" Daddy calls from the hall. "Where are you?"

I am invisible. I lie down with my knees bent. His footsteps scrape across the rug toward Mama and me. They stop right on the other side of the curtain.

"IRIS!"

I hold my breath and lift the hem. The shiny toes of his black boots are so close I smell shoe polish. My ceiling jiggles. The lid of the coffin creaks open. Daddy takes a deep breath and holds it forever. It's so quiet. Just the three of us at home together, until the doorbell chimes and Daddy turns and walks away.

I reach under the curtain and pull the stool into my playhouse. I try to sit on it, but I'm too tall. So I drag it out, stand on top, and look into the creamy box with thick silver handles that has Mama inside.

She's wearing her dark green dress with covered buttons. Her eyes are shut. I know she can't play our game now, but I lean down anyway and blink at her like we did at the sanatorium when her throat got too sore for her to talk. I'd blink all different ways and she'd blink back exactly the same. We thought it was funny. You can just tell from a person's eyes if they think something is as funny as you do.

When Mama got so sick that breathing made her cough, she quit that, too. I tried to stop breathing like her, but I couldn't. A person can't make her own heart stop beating either—God has to help you do that.

It's good now because Mama isn't coughing. She must be so glad.

Her fingers, folded on her chest, don't move when I poke them. Her shiny hair, the same dark brown as mine, is tucked under her head. It looks lumpy to lie on, but I don't tell her, because dead people can't move anymore.

Her feet are under the part of the coffin lid that won't

open. I can't see her shoes, which is bad because Daddy sells shoes. A person wearing the proper shoes for every occasion is real important to him.

I need to know which pair she is wearing for her walk into heaven. I sneak into Mama's empty bedroom. A sachet of dead rose petals hangs by a silver ribbon on the wardrobe knob. I count her shoes—black pumps, black boots, tan and white, brown with high heels and elastic sides, gray, and ivory with buttons. All six pairs are here—one for every year since I was born.

"IRIS!"

My hand jerks. I knock Mama's shoes from their neat row.

Daddy marches up to me, his watch chain bouncing on his coat. I smell his pipe. He closes the wardrobe almost before I can get my fingers out of the way. "You made a mess."

I feel hot. I don't look up. "Is Mama . . . barefoot?"

"The guests are here. Get off the floor."

"But . . ."

Daddy turns and points at me with his pipe. "And be polite."

CHAPTER 1

APRIL 1926

I pull my hand from our mailbox, the letter bent in my fingers, my mind reeling. An official letter for Daddy from a *doctor*. A bud of panic starts to grow in me.

My father is sick.

I drift up our endless front walk, turn a slow circle on the porch before I open the front door. Up and down our street is empty and deathly still, like my heart.

I slide the letter under the mail-order catalogs on his desk and sit on the edge of the divan. He went to a doctor in another town to protect me from the bad news, to avoid the Atchison party line, the gossip. The gaping black hole of our fireplace stares at me. I stare right back.

My worst fear, that I am going to lose him the way I did Mama, is sealed in that envelope. I picture his coffin in the parlor, just like hers almost ten years ago. I squeeze my eyes shut to crush the scene and try to breathe.

A family of wrens chatters in our lilac bush, unaware that my family of two is about to become one. In a moment I'm standing at his desk. I retrieve the envelope and hold it to the light, but I can't see through. I reach for the letter opener. With one simple slice I could know the truth.

No, not yet. Not by myself.

I sit in the desk chair, my head down, and listen to Mama and Daddy's old anniversary clock on the mantel chop the silence to bits.

"Leroy," I whisper into the empty room. "I need to talk to you."

I fumble out the front door, trip over my books still piled by the mailbox. I stop halfway to Leroy's house. He won't be home from work yet. He's still delivering groceries.

God . . .

I stand—a scarecrow lost in the middle of the street.

Maybe I'll go see Daddy at work, just peek at him through the window doing his normal things—talking up customers, ringing the cash register with a flashy grin, waltzing ladies and their pocketbooks around the shoe displays.

I turn toward town. Or maybe I'll go in the store and say, *You got mail today from Wellsford, Missouri.* Or *Do you know a doctor named Avery Nesbitt? He sent you a letter.*

Or maybe I won't.

I stop outside the store—my reflection mixed with the

arrangement of two-tone spectator dress shoes and fancy spring pumps inside. Daddy stands alone at the open cash register, counting the day's profits. His back definitely looks different—thinner and more stooped than when I left for school this morning. I step back from the glass. If I don't move, keep glued to this moment, to this spot on the sidewalk, time will stop and there will be no future to lose him in.

He turns suddenly, squints through the window. He knows he's being watched. I have no choice. I grab the handle and push the door open. The perfume of leather and glue and vinegar glass cleaner makes my eyes water.

"Hello." I sound croaky, cautious.

He nods as he anchors a stack of receipts with a green glass paperweight. He does not ask what I'm doing here.

"How are you today?"

He looks up sharply. "Fine!"

I twist my hair, helpless for what to say next. The backroom curtain hangs open. Daddy's shoe repairman, Carl, has left for the day. "Do you . . . uh, need help with anything?"

"Nope."

"How are the new Kansas City store plans coming along?" I wince. The question is so out of the blue, so idiotic and phony-sounding.

He shrugs, which could mean *Okay* or *Can't you see I'm busy* or *Get lost, Iris.*

I turn, bump the counter. Shoeboxes clatter to the floor. "Oh, I'm sorry, I just . . ." I straighten the mess, swipe my eyes. "I'll see you soon—around five, then."

He glances at the clock and says not one word when I walk out the door.

"Bye, Daddy."

On the way home I plan how I'll move the letter to the top of the mail stack so he can't miss it. I'll be right there to help him when he reads it.

I shudder. A long-ago scene pops into my mind. At Mama's funeral he said "I'm sorry" to her doctor. I thought it was strange, even then, him apologizing for her not getting well. That's why he got rid of most all her belongings except the secretary desk, as though her hatpins and stockings had tuberculosis too. To him, illness is weakness. He still stiffens when I sneeze, scowls at every cough.

My hands turn icy. I cannot imagine how he will ever admit that being sick could happen to him.

But now he will finally need me for something . . . to help him get well.

My eyes fill with tears. He has *got* to get well.

My father sorts the mail, gives me a glance when he spots the letter, but doesn't open it. All through dinner—round steak and beets that I cannot eat—I long for him to ask me his usual string of tired questions: *How is piano coming along, Iris?* I don't take piano anymore. *How are your marks in ancient history?* That was last quarter. But he just chews, dabs his whiskers with the napkin, and reads the classified ads neatly folded by his plate.

It's maddening. But tonight, if he'd only ask, I'd answer his questions ten times in detail. I'd act interested in anything—used cars, the latest reverse-leather boot styles, profit projections, even his gaudy girlfriend, Celeste.

When the dishes are done, while I pretend to do my Latin homework, he sits at his desk studying the shoe section of a Sears and Roebuck catalog, complaining about "cheap mail-order shoes that don't hold up to the elements." Finally he slices the envelope with his brass knife. I cross my arms and wait. He reads the letter twice, moving his head ever so slightly back and forth as the news pulls him along. Daddy clears his throat and rubs his whiskers, his face flushed. He slides the medical report in his drawer, drums his fingers. "I'm going by Celeste's," he remarks without looking up. "I'll be later than usual." He scrapes his chair back and walks out.

The engine revs. The car door slams.

I burst into tears on the porch swing, my heart a knot.

"Meet me, Leroy, please," I whisper into the phone minutes later. "Our spot."

And he does.

A breeze lifts wisps of his messy red hair. He picks chips of dusty green paint off the picnic table we always sit on while I spill my story. "He just left to tell Celeste . . . *first*." I bury my face.

"Who's she?"

"You know . . . his latest lady friend."

Leroy leans back on his elbows, studies the dusky sky.

"You're saying he just rushed out the door to tell his girl-friend that he is going to die?"

"Yes."

"Uh . . . Iris?" Leroy bumps my arm. "How do you know it's a medical report? Did you *read* it? I mean, you've already turned him into a memory!"

My insides feel wild. We sit silent a miserably long time. "You've got this all blown up. It could be something else." He puts his handkerchief in my hand, swallows hard. "This death stuff you always dream up . . . you're kinda morbid."

The word settles over me. Something shifts inside. I swipe my cheeks. "Did I hear you call me *morbid*?"

"Yeah."

"So just one stupid word explains *me*?" I take a sharp breath, wave my hands. "My father is dying, but oh . . . never mind, Iris is just being her old morbid self again!"

Leroy doesn't move.

My words crackle between us. "Shut up about stuff you don't know, Leroy. Maybe you forgot that I only have one person left to make a family with. Not like you." I count on my fingers. "Let's see—two parents, three sisters, dogs, rabbits, and God knows what else. So, of course, *you* wouldn't get it. But in my *family*, everybody's dead except Daddy. I *have* to care about him. He's *it*!"

"Iris?" Leroy looks at me, amazed, and with something else . . . awe? "How'd you do it?"

I lash the word. "What?"

"Change so fast from morbid . . . to *mad*?"

"Shut up, Leroy."

"Wow. I mean it. Mad's good. Don't *you* shut up, Iris. Stay mad. It beats morbid any day."

We sit there staring at each other, but for some reason this silence between us feels strong and full and worth listening to.

"You've gotta read it," Leroy says finally. "Maybe he's a doctor of something else, like a reverend, and your dad's getting married, or . . ."

A crow hops by pecking the new grass. It looks up at me with a beady eye, cocks its head—*Iris Baldwin, go read that letter.*

Leroy slides off the table, grabs my arm. "Let's go!"

"Reading someone's mail is a crime," I whisper as we rush across my front porch.

"I know that."

"So's breaking into somebody's desk," I say, holding the front door open for Leroy.

He smiles down at me and says in a singsong voice, "Let's do please shut up."

It feels like a little crime just having him in the parlor. He has never stepped foot inside when nobody else is home. He seems taller in here than outside. His eyes sweep the room, rest on Daddy's desk.

I pull the drawer handle. Without stopping to think, I open the envelope. A photograph of me flutters to the floor. I turn to Leroy. "Oh, my God, it's not Daddy who's dying, it's *me*! The doctor could tell just from my picture."

Leroy's eyes are saucers. "Iris! You're nuts." He holds the picture to the light. "You don't look sick, you look . . ." His neck turns pink, he points to the paper. "Just read it out loud."

I take a deep breath.

April 21, 1926

Dear Mr. Charles Baldwin,

Thank you for your response to my inquiry in the Atchison Daily Globe. As stated, the position includes housekeeping duties, daily nursing care, and companionship for my elderly mother, who is ill and confined to a wheelchair . . .

My ears ring. I can't hear the words. I turn the page over, certain I am reading the wrong side.

. . . room and board will be provided . . .

My voice wavers. Leroy touches my elbow.

Enclosed is the rail schedule to

Wellsford and the photograph of Iris you sent.

Employment will begin June 1 and continue through Labor Day.

Cordially,
Avery Nesbitt, M.D.

I hear Leroy's breath quicken, feel him watch me fold the letter and scrape the drawer shut. The words punch through the haunted fog in my mind. Daddy's not sick. He's not dying. He's *fine*. He's launched this secret plan so he and Celeste can go to Kansas City for the summer and open the new store without me.

In a flash I am outside and halfway down the block.

Leroy is right behind me, but I do not turn around. One sorry look, one wrong remark from him, and I'll shatter. I dread that he's going to try and cheer me up, gloss over the fact that my perfectly healthy father has mistaken me for a piece of furniture that doesn't fit in his house, his life, anymore. If Leroy says one tiny nice thing about Daddy, I swear I will explode.

"Iris, slow down."

I don't. I could march straight across the Missouri River right now and not get wet.

"Iris. Hold up for a second."

I stomp to the end of another block. Then stop with my back to him. I plant my feet—one, two.

"WHAT?"

He walks a few steps ahead and turns back to me. He opens his mouth, but I speak before he can make things worse. "Don't tell me this isn't pathetic. Don't you dare. I've just committed a crime to find out that that *sneak* has been planning to get rid of me, for God's sake. It's not *fine* . . . it's . . . he's . . ."

Leroy's face is dead serious. He clenches his fists, then levels his dark eyes on mine. "This is the way he always treats you. You've said it yourself a thousand times. I'll tell you what I think you should do."

I cover my ears. Here it comes.

Leroy growls the words, "Tell him no."

CHAPTER 2

JUNE 1926

I hate my feet.

They're stuck inside these prissy suede boots with gros-grain ribbon ties. The boots pinch. They squeak. They're just big walking advertisements for Baldwin's Shoes.

The little girl across from me cannot keep her eyes off them. She looks from my feet to my face and back again. "How old are you?" she asks.

"Almost sixteen."

"I'm eight." She finishes cutting a family of paper dolls from the *Ladies' Home Journal* and lines them up across the seat of the train. She puts me in charge of the father. I am to hold him upright when it's his turn to talk, even though his head has not survived her scissors. Her mother gives me a resigned smile and hands me a peppermint. She wears nice tan boots with hook-and-eye closures.

The girl acts out a paper doll drama about children begging their parents for a puppy. She hop-walks the family members across the upholstered seat, changing voices for each character. She seems to know exactly what each person in a family would say and do. And naturally, the kind and perfect Daddy finally surprises them with a dog.

The paper father in my hand is headless, but not heartless, I think.

The opposite of mine.

I wave out the train window when the girl and her mother exit at Clearview. I sit back, caved into the space between my shoulders, staring at my boots. What an imbecile in diapers I was to believe I had a real role in my play-act family.

Besides my feet, the other part of me I hate is the part that didn't even try, that can't say no to anyone about anything. I'm sorry, Leroy. I'm a chicken.

I inherited it from my father.

For one whole month after the letter came I rubbed the blister between Daddy and me with questions. At dinner I would needle him about my responsibilities at the store this summer. At breakfast I'd say things like, "I can't wait to help with the window dressings in Kansas City. We should plant zinnias in pots by the front door." But he just rattled the front page of the *Atchison Daily Globe* as though it had wilted under his fierce attention. He clucked over his cornflakes and pecked at his toast. He did everything but be honest with me.

Carl, our shoe repairman, used to shake his head and, when he thought I couldn't hear, mutter under his breath, "Charles Baldwin is a bullshit salesman."

He's right. *I* am one of Daddy's best customers. But then I'm just full of a different kind of manure—chicken. Did I refuse when he finally tried to sell Wellsford as a grand opportunity?

"It's lovely, Iris."

"It's not on the map."

"Avery Nesbitt is a *doctor.* You'll meet important people, cultivate friends, learn housekeeping and sick care."

"Dr. Nesbitt thinks I already know those things," I had answered flatly. Daddy must not have noticed that our housekeeper, Mrs. Andrews, cooked and cleaned; she didn't *teach* it.

He said I would be bored in Kansas City. . . . *Bored?*

I stare out the window into fields shimmering in the afternoon sun. Rows of spring wheat closest to the track whiz past us. Farther out they spin as though pulled by the train. Farther still, crumpled cloud pillows are tossed across the horizon. We rattle over bridges and whistle our way into stops with nothing more than a crooked water spigot and a painted plank sign: Newbridge, Tarkio.

When we pull away, I see that cows are corralled where the rest of the towns should be. They look grand wearing their shiny hides of spotted black and white, chocolate brown and tan. We turn a curve, cross another bridge. The whistle shrieks. The brakes scream. We jerk—rock—jerk to a dead stop in the middle of nowhere.

I lower the window, gulp the sooty air, my heart pounding. There's nothing but whipped prairie grass and cotton-woods.

A mangy little dog trips down the aisle, chased by a porter who yells as he passes, "Don't worry folks. We just hit a cow."

I wiggle my toes; hear the puny creaks of my bleached leather boots, ghosts of the animals they once were. I remember Carl saying that a self-respecting cow should resist becoming suede.

Men gather outside to stretch and light their pipes. Ladies hold their skirts against the wind. An old couple shares a tin of cookies.

The train is hot, but I stay put. I'm closer to Leroy and Atchison in here. And I am *not* going to think about that cow, the way I am also *not* thinking about Dr. Avery Nesbitt and his half-dead mother. The train purrs in place. I raise the window to keep out the grasshoppers and grit.

I know only one detail about Wellsford: Dr. Nesbitt has a black fountain pen and perfect handwriting. The rest of him shows up in my imagination. He's a tall know-it-all, wide around the middle with a black caterpillar mustache. He is not one bit interested in me.

Their two-story white house will be surrounded by elm trees and a wrap-around porch. The dining room shades will be drawn because it's used as his mother's bedroom. She's shriveled and whiskery, bent over in her wheelchair.

The kitchen is as sterile as a doctor's office, with a jar of tongue depressors where the sugar canister should be.

My stomach churns. I can't see *me* in there anywhere.

I can't see myself anywhere, at all.

The train gets underway. Clothesline poles replace windmills. In minutes we glide into the depot.

I wipe my eyes. The porter knocks on my compartment. "Wellsford."

I grab my pocketbook and bag and suddenly I know what part of me *will* stay on the train. I walk out in my stockings, leave my boots hiding under the seat, ashamed, like they should be, to step into cow country.

The depot is painted dark green with peeling red trim around the windows. A wooden sign reads: AMERICAN RR EXPRESS AGENCY. There are barrels, a blackboard listing the rail schedule, and freight carts pulled alongside the platform.

I squint into the wind and hop from the bottom step in my stocking feet.

My make-believe Dr. Nesbitt is nowhere in sight.

"Heard you killed a fella."

The speaker is right behind me. I wheel around and stare into a wide, windburned face with dark piggy eyes.

"What?"

"You killed a bum." The man's tone says, *Don't you even know what you did?*

"Sir?"

He answers as if I'm slow. "It wasn't a boveen accident. Not a moo cow, missy. A man was kilt."

"Boveen?"

He's clearly amused by the confusion he's creating. "Wasn't a cow, like they claimed." He glances down the track. "Doc Avery was supposed to pick you up, but he had to take off to pronounce him, or at least the remainin' parts of him, dead."

"Who?"

"The hobo fishin' off the bridge." He glances at the passenger car. "I see you picked up his mutt."

The hobo's muddy stray has limped off the train and is sniffing my trunk.

The piggy man looks me up and down, twice. He smirks at my stocking feet, and motions toward a horse-drawn wagon parked by the FREIGHT ROOM sign.

I stand stapled to the platform.

He raises his eyebrows, as if he wonders if I'll know the answer, and asks, "You *are* Iris Baldwin, ain't ya, *Miss* Iris Baldwin?"

I barely nod.

"Cecil Deets." He says both names with an odd, drawn out *e* sound like he thinks I'm part deaf.

He takes forever putting my trunk in the wagon. He spits, rubs his palm on his overalls stretched tight across his belly, and tugs at his crotch. He glances again at my feet, then at me. I turn my back, dig my old shoes from my bag, and put them on as the train pulls out.

Wellsford appears on the other side of the tracks. There's a stone hotel, three steeples, a barber shop, and a Standard Oil gas pump in front of a dry goods store. There are houses and what looks to be a school next to a tiny court-house.

Cecil Deets lumbers onto the wagon seat, looks down at me. I get goose bumps, even on the inside. He scratches his fat neck, lays his hand palm-up where I am supposed to sit on the bench. "So, get in." He motions toward the depot outhouse with its door hanging open. "Unless you'd like to use the . . . little girl's room. We've got a long ride together."

"But where's . . . ?"

"Ain't you been hired by Doctor Avery Nesbitt?" He sounds irritated. "Then that's where we're headed, Miss Iris Baldwin. To your new boss."

I climb onto the wooden seat, scoot as far from him as possible. We circle the depot and head out on a wide dirt road. My stomach is a knot. My trunk bucks and rattles behind me. "Where does he live?"

"Miz Nesbitt's farm. What's he payin' ya?"

I ignore the money question. "He's married?"

Cecil snorts—something between a burp and a laugh. But he doesn't answer.

"Oh, I know, you mean Mrs. Nesbitt—Dr. Nesbitt's mother."

"Queer," he says, and then laughs again. "Yes, indeed." He gives me a long glance. "Doc Avery's been living here with his *mama* since his brother was shot by the Germans. I'm their tenant—rent their land."

I don't know what to say, so I shut up. Talking to him feels rotten.

The horse lopes along with its tail cranking against the flies. We pass a brick silo, a dilapidated barn, and a rusted plow choked by vines. So is this Daddy's idea of a "lovely town"—full of creeps and strays and dead bums?

I'll have to ask him *all* about that when he comes to visit like he promised. That'll be the day.

The wagon hits a bump. I knock into Cecil and bite my tongue. The sting fills my face. I taste blood. I'm five years old again, riding home from Mama's sanatorium with Daddy, and for an indescribable moment I wish like anything that this was then.

Cecil's knuckles are fat. He's got spots on the backs of his hands and no wedding ring. I picture the little girl from the train. I wonder how she would act out *this* play. She wouldn't, because in her life stories make sense, they have a point and a happy ending.

"Dot's *my* girl," Cecil says out of the blue.

"Y-your wife?"

He swipes his nose. "My daughter. Thirteen." He twists his neck, leers at me. "*You* look closer to seventeen."

I don't correct him.

"Dot's mother . . . passed." Cecil looks skyward. I follow his gaze. Hawks dive overhead. This land does not look that different from the surroundings of Atchison, but I feel like Persephone, in our Greek mythology unit, when she was banished to live in the underworld with Hades.

Cecil yanks the reins. We roll past a mailbox, past a telephone pole, and up a long driveway. Ahead is a pale stucco house with a low green roof. It has cement steps to the front stoop and a pair of slanted storm cellar doors buried in the yard.

I hop off the seat onto a patch of gravel. Chickens watch Cecil jerk my trunk up the steps. He opens the front door and yells real light and friendly, "Yoo-hoo, Mrs. Nesbitt, Miss Iris Baldwin is here, at your service!"

Cecil lugs my trunk inside. He turns to me with that shifty smile and sweeps his arm.

When I step in, he steps out. He huffs off the front stoop and into his wagon. He clucks the horse and hisses at me from a swirl of dust, "Shut the goddamned door!"

I close it so fast, not even a shadow has time to escape.

CHAPTER 3

I blink at the gloom. My trunk, sitting crossways on the carpet runner, looks confused, as though it's been delivered to the wrong threshold.

My collar is tight. I can't peep *Hello?* or *Anybody home?*

I hear the tap and rustle of branches sweeping the roof. The doors along the hall are shut except one. The walls creak and moan *Go . . . away . . . now . . .*

Morbid moves in.

I imagine Mrs. Nesbitt is in one of these shrouded rooms, dead in bed. I shiver, picturing the grim dry seam of her mouth, her stiff fingers the color of tallow. She has died while her son is out pronouncing somebody else dead . . . and somehow Cecil knew it. He knew exactly what I was walking into. That's why he swore and raced away.

I grip my handbag and creep down the dark hall, clear my throat and whisper, "I'm here. Iris Baldwin has arrived." I listen for a gasp, a whimper.

Nothing.

I step through the open door.

Flies caught behind the heavy parlor drapes buzz helplessly. My slate-blue dress dissolves in the gloom. The wallpaper is faded rose bunches tied with poison ivy. A hulking upright piano fills one wall. The keys look like gritted yellow teeth. At least if Mrs. Nesbitt is dead, I can go home.

A dingy dish towel covers a painting above the piano. I imagine a skeleton hand reaching from behind, pinching the cloth, and lifting it.

I have absolutely no idea what to do, so I sit on the edge of the divan and stare into the painted black eyes of two figurines facing me from their little wall sconce. Their bored expressions ask, *Why are you here?*

I want to go sit on my trunk, but I can't make myself move.

Daddy lied. This isn't a house in a town full of important people. This is not like any farmhouse I've ever read about, heard about, or imagined. Farmhouses are supposed to be bright and sunny with muddy galoshes on the step. There are supposed to be litters of kittens on the porch, big soft chairs, and kitchens that smell like fried chicken.

Or maybe Daddy didn't exactly *lie*—he just didn't care,

wasn't interested enough to find out the truth about this haunted funeral home.

Stale wood smoke gusts down the chimney. A slice of late afternoon sun appears on the floor across the room. Behind it is a partially open door and another room cast in deep shadow. The pool of sunlight swims, as if the wind has blown it onto the rug.

From miles off a train whistles. I know what Leroy would do. He'd hitchhike to the depot and jump a train home. But then, he'd have a home to go to.

I stare at the spot—a glowing puddle of melted sun. Blown grit ticks the windows. I hear a slight shuffle, a tap. My scalp tingles. Out of nowhere a slipper and the tip of a cane step into the light.

My hands fly up. *"Ah?"* I look at the owner of the feet.

"Miss Baldwin?" says a tiny old woman.

"Oh!" I scramble to stand. My hat and pocketbook thump on the floor.

"Hello, Iris."

"M-Mrs. Nesbitt?" Every part of me trembles. "It's so dark in here. . . . I thought . . ."

She walks to the window, her back straight, her chin up, and raises the shade. The shawl wrapping her narrow shoulders blazes in the afternoon sunlight. It matches her slippers—gold silk, embroidered with crimson chrysanthemums and lanterns.

She turns to me. Plants her cane. Her eyes are fiery, brilliant little headlamps. "Shocked by me, are you?"

"I'm sorry, but I thought that you . . ."

"Were an ailing invalid?" She looks heavenward behind wire-rimmed glasses. "That son of mine . . ." She glances at the piano. "Here's my theory, Miss Baldwin. Piano tuners hear only the flat notes. Without sin, preachers have no livelihood. English teachers thrill at a flaw in a freshly diagrammed sentence." She studies me and clears her throat.

"Ma'am?"

"And *doctors*, like my dear Avery," she taps her cane to emphasize every word, "find half-dead invalids where there are none." She pauses a moment and says, "After your journey I trust you could use tea."

She grips her cane with crippled fingers, watches me intently. Does she wonder if I am also the type who will find her flaws, her limp, and nothing else?

She steadies herself. "Meet Henry, my *assistant*." She wags her fancy cane. "He's bamboo. Quite elegant, although a bit too tall for me. Of Japanese descent, so conversation is a trifle difficult." She winks.

I swear, in my whole life nobody has ever winked at me.

"So if I've misplaced Henry and he doesn't come find me on his own"—she raises her eyebrows—"you'll know who I'm talking about and will be kind enough to retrieve him for me."

I follow her as she makes her way across the hall and into the dining room. Her elegantly outfitted feet seem a bit less crippled than her hands. "You're lagging behind, Henry," she fusses, giving her cane a snappy *hurry up* tap.

We raise the shades. A long mirror with a carved ebony frame hangs over the buffet. The table has been pushed aside to make room for a bed—my bed, I suppose, with a crocheted bedspread and monogrammed pillow case. Next to it is a night stand and a small chest of drawers.

"Miss Baldwin, I am very embarrassed by your accommodations—sleeping in the dining room, for God's sake! We will treat this space as your private domain."

I nod, remembering that an hour ago I had *her* living in the dining room.

She slides a crooked finger over the table. "Oh, yes, we must discuss dust."

"Ma'am?"

"Why, I ask you, on the Seventh Day, didn't the Creator pave the roads of Wellsford, Missouri, instead of resting? Rain tames the stuff, but not for long. So does frost, but"—she glances out the window—"not in June. Every day—several times a day—I will impose on you to dust.

"My glasses are the worst." She works the spectacles off her face and hands them to me. They weigh absolutely nothing. Mrs. Nesbitt fishes a hankie from her cuff. "Keep it. As you can see, my hands are lame. I simply can't clean my glasses like I used to."

I wipe the lenses and hold them to the light for her inspection.

She tilts her face to me. She wears lipstick, a bit of rouge, and perfume. Her bun is several shades of silver held with a tortoiseshell hair fork.

I bend over, hold my breath, and ever so slowly pull the wire earpieces into place, careful to avoid knocking her earrings. My hands are clumsier than hers. When I try to center the lenses, I bang her cheek with the back of my hand and gasp right in her face. "Oh . . . I . . . I'm so horrible at . . ." I look away.

Do not cry. Do not cry.

"Avery swears the trickiest surgery he does is removing his patients' eyeglasses. And even harder than removal is putting the darned things back on."

Mrs. Nesbitt bows her head. The moment collects itself. "Thank you for your help, Iris," she says the way someone might end a prayer.

I follow Mrs. Nesbitt and Henry into the kitchen.

She smiles and points to a small, papery lump on a saucer by the sink. "One can *always* squeeze another cup of tea from a used tea bag."

"Yes, ma'am."

"We get our tea bags from New York. Avery's dear friend Marsden sends them."

The kitchen is an aboveground food cellar with windows and a back door. The cabinets are lined with jars of string beans and jam. Next to a bread box is a tin of saltines and what looks to be a fresh pie wrapped in waxed paper. The table holds a magnifying glass, copies of *The Kansas City Star,* and a folded paper fan. There's a telephone, an ice box, a gas range, and a shotgun propped by the back door.

Mrs. Nesbitt is watching me. "Do you want the truth?" she says.

"Ma'am?"

"Avery and I don't cook. His patients who can't pay— most of them, actually—keep us fed. But I miss the smells,

the art of it. Of course, nobody in Wellsford would understand me on that." She doesn't ask if I can cook. I think she
has already figured that one out.

"Would you like me to fix the tea?" I ask bravely, glanc-
ing at two dainty, but dusty, teacups on the counter. I'd
like to tell her I'm better at touching china than human
beings. I'm better with boiling water than warm people.

Perched on the chair like an exotic little bird, Mrs. Nesbitt watches me fill the kettle and light the burner.

"I suppose you had electricity at home in Atchison," she
says.

"Yes, ma'am."

"Avery has electricity at his medical office in town,
but it's not here yet." She sighs. "I'm so very sorry for the
inconvenience, Miss Baldwin."

I'm at a loss for words. My inconvenience is not something I've ever considered. Until now, no one has ever
mentioned my *inconvenience* about anything. My father never
asked: *Iris, will spending the summer in Wellsford, Missouri, without electricity be an inconvenience for you?* or *Will wearing these prissy suede boots
around the store inconvenience your toes?*

I answer her questions about my train trip and explain
how the cow turned out to be a dead bum. "Mr. Deets said
Dr. Nesbitt had to go pronounce the man dead." A shadow
crosses her face. I can't tell if it's about Cecil, the hobo, or
something else entirely.

Mrs. Nesbitt explains her son's schedule. "On evenings
and weekends Avery sees folks at our office here." She nods
toward a bolted door off the kitchen. I learn they moved

seven years ago from St. Louis, and that Cecil's wife, Pansy, used to do their housekeeping. Mrs. Nesbitt shakes her head. "She was a troubled woman." She doesn't mention that Pansy has passed, nor does she speak of her other son, the one Cecil told me was killed in the war.

I watch her slanted, swollen fingers barely manage the teacup. I'm bewildered as to if, or how, I should help.

Mrs. Nesbitt cocks her ear. I listen too, but don't hear a thing except the squeak of a windmill through the screen door.

She plants Henry and stands. "Avery's coming!" She pats her hair, adjusts the remarkable shawl over her black housecoat, and positions her tiny hands on the cane handle.

I stand too, smooth my skirt, and fold my napkin as small as I can. Beside her I feel like something giant and dull.

Mrs. Nesbitt's eyes dart from her cane to the window. She works her mouth like an actress silently rehearsing her lines.

I hear the crunch of car tires. My stomach flutters.

Mrs. Nesbitt gives me an anxious smile. Is she embarrassed of me . . . *for* me? She straightens her spine.

A car door slams. Footsteps. A dog yowls. Chickens screech, as through the back door walks Dr. Avery Nesbitt.

CHAPTER 4

He swipes a glance at me then fixes on his mother with an expression of sheer astonishment.

"Mother?"

He starts toward her, I think to grab her arm, but stops himself, steps back. He looks around the room, then rests his gaze on Henry. Dr. Nesbitt is slight, clean-shaven, pale-haired, about Daddy's age, and only a bit taller than me.

Behind him limps a creature—a cross between a long-legged skunk, a flop-eared coyote, and a weasel.

The dead hobo's dog.

Mrs. Nesbitt's gaze bounces between her son and the dog. *"Avery?"* she says in an exact imitation of him.

Dr. Nesbitt stares at her slippers and shawl.

She pats my arm. "Oh, I'm so sorry. Avery, please meet Miss Iris Baldwin. We're having tea."

He nods, smiles politely. "Welcome to Wellsford." His gaze returns immediately to his mother and her cane. "I haven't seen that cane in years."

"My *chair's* in the bedroom," she says firmly.

Dr. Nesbitt looks at me and raises one eyebrow a fraction of a fraction of an inch. "I see." He gets a bowl of water and sets it on the floor. The dog drinks, then flops on its side. I stare and hold my breath, waiting for the next shallow rise and fall of its ribs. "So you've brought us a patient?" Mrs. Nesbitt remarks.

"I found her when I filed that poor man's death certificate at the depot. She belonged to the hobo. Needs stitches." He turns to me. "Miss Baldwin, what a harrowing afternoon *you* must have had. Was the entire train in an uproar?"

"No. They said we'd hit a cow."

He nods, his face grim. "That old vagabond was probably deaf as stone, fishing for dinner." He sighs. "I've witnessed hundreds of exits from life . . . some are just sadder, more empty, than others."

He checks his watch, unbolts his office door, then turns to face us. "I hate to interrupt your tea time, but while we've got daylight left, I could use your help with this pup."

He rubs the dog's ears, then picks her up. "First, Mother, we need your help with a name. Having a proper name might help her survive the night, and you're just the person for it." We follow as he carries the dog to his examining table and lights two kerosene lamps. He places a chair for his mother by the dog's head.

Mrs. Nesbitt studies the trembling animal, caked in mud and dried blood, and announces, "Marie!"

Dr. Nesbitt looks as if he hasn't heard her right.

"Marie?"

"Marie," she repeats, riveting us with those fiery eyes. "I've thought about it and I like it."

Dr. Nesbitt lifts one ear flap and says, "Okay, Marie, just keep still while I examine you." He gently probes down her sides, her legs, her tail, all the while stroking her and crooning, "You're strong. You're going to be fine."

His tender voice, the smell of rubbing alcohol so like Mama's sanatorium, and Marie lying helpless on the table mix together inside me and I can't help it, I start crying. I sniff and dab, and soak Mrs. Nesbitt's hankie.

"Tears bathe the heart," she remarks. She and Dr. Nesbitt wait until I'm through, as if it's the most natural thing in the world to let someone finish crying. "It's a miracle," he says, turning to his mother. "I can't find a flea or a tick anywhere, but . . ." He holds up Marie's tail—a muddy, broken feather. "We'll have to amputate this piece."

I look away, praying I won't have to touch it.

"She's also got a slew of cuts that need stitching. Iris, could you please get the strainer from the kitchen cabinet just left of the sink."

Strainer? I rummage in the kitchen, return to the office with it. He's holding a dark brown bottle with a stopper.

The label says: Ether. "We'll soak cotton with this and line the bottom of the strainer. Then you hold it over her nose."

Marie looks up at me and blinks, her eyes as watery as mine. Mrs. Nesbitt pats my arm. "What in the world would we do without you, Iris?"

Dr. Nesbitt opens the window, then the ether bottle. Crickets, tree frogs, and a chorus of cows join us in the room. The ether smells sickeningly sweet. I hold my breath, take the strainer from Dr. Nesbitt, and put it over Marie's nose.

Her whiskers poke this way and that through the mesh. Her breathing slows. I glance at Dr. Nesbitt, absolutely certain I've killed her. But he's busy cleaning and assessing her wounds.

I feel clammy, light-headed.

Don't watch him.

Think of something else, anything else . . .

What's Leroy doing at this moment? Missing me maybe? What about Daddy? Hmm . . . he's huddled with Celeste in Kansas City. They're planning their fancy window displays for Petticoat Lane. I wonder what county my suede boots have traveled to by now. I think of the paper doll family on the train. I wonder how that little girl would act out *this* "getting a puppy" story.

Marie whimpers. I jump. Dr. Nesbitt, in the middle of removing the broken tail, instructs me to shake four more drops of ether on the strainer cotton. Mrs. Nesbitt sits at the end of the table, cupping one of Marie's front paws in her hands. I think she'd hold my hand too if she could.

A few drops of ether dissolve in thin air before they hit the floor. But overall I manage without spilling the whole bottle or fainting.

Mrs. Nesbitt watches her son's every stitch, but I can't. I concentrate on reading the eye chart on the wall across the room and alphabetizing the labels on his shelf full of ointments and adhesive tape.

When he's finished and it's finally time to remove the ether for good, we wrap Marie in a blanket. "She can sleep in here tonight," he says as we lower her to the floor. "By the window. She probably needs the stars for a good night's sleep."

In the kitchen lamplight I could die. My cotton dress is completely stuck to me with sweat. I cross my arms, huddle on the chair.

My back and neck ache. My stomach rumbles. I've lost all track of time. I can't recall how or where this day started. In fact, I can't say exactly if I am the same person who started it.

Dr. Nesbitt lights the gas range, unwraps a chicken potpie and places it in the oven.

"What else?" Mrs. Nesbitt asks, looking over a row of canning jars. "Succotash? Stewed tomatoes?"

Dr. Nesbitt rolls his eyes. "With the afternoon I've had, the last thing I want to look at is a stewed tomato!"

"Careful of your wicked sense of humor, or Iris will be on the next train." Mrs. Nesbitt smiles and claps.

"We need brandy! Lord knows we've all had an extraordinary day. Iris, could you please get the decanter and three snifters from your *bedroom*? They're on the buffet. Oh, and a candleholder off the table. This is a night for celebration. By the way, Avery, I told Iris we'd eat in the kitchen instead of the dining room while she's with us."

Dr. Nesbitt's expression seems to say, *What? We* never *eat in the dining room.*

When I return with the brandy, he pours a few sips in my glass. "Today, besides the hobo's accident, I had to remove a decades-old plug of earwax, pull three black teeth, and—"

Mrs. Nesbitt makes a face and cuts him off. "Thank you, dear."

I place the holder on the kitchen table and light the candle. Dr. Nesbitt stretches. So does the flame. I take my first sip of brandy—a swallow of liquid fire. We sit around the little table. The kitchen smells like chicken after all.

"By the way, Mother, did I mention that you look ravishing this evening?"

Mrs. Nesbitt tips her cane. "Thank you, Avery."

"Dad bought that cane and shawl for you, didn't he?" he says.

She strokes the silk embroidery and smiles. "The Japanese Bazaar at the World's Fair—St. Louis, 1904."

"We can shorten the cane a bit, if you plan to use it," Dr. Nesbitt says, standing. He unbuttons his coat, opens the oven.

"Yes, I introduced Iris to Henry this afternoon."

"Who?" Dr. Nesbitt says immediately, turning to his mother. He raises his eyebrows, potholder in hand. "Henry?"

"Henry!" Mrs. Nesbitt says. "My cane."

A smile twitches his lips. He dishes up the potpie. "You've named the cane . . . ?"

"Henry."

"It isn't exactly a *Japanese* name, Mother."

"Well, it goes well with Marie!"

We eat a few moments in silence. I don't know what to add to the conversation. Would Dr. Nesbitt be interested in hearing about people's corn and bunion problems when they're being fitted for shoes? Well, actually, maybe he would! But I keep my mouth shut.

"I also had to convince Vivian Eckles that there's nothing medically I can do for her hiccups," he says. "I told her to go home, put a silver knife in a glass of water, and drink it upside down with a paper sack over her head. And if that doesn't work, I prescribed biting the ends of her little fingers and picturing an old gray horse, or, as a last resort, passionate kissing!"

My mouthful of succotash is ready to explode.

"Avery! After that session with the ether and then the succotash, you're going to kill Iris!"

Dr. Nesbitt nods an apology my way, then smiles and taps the side of his head. He holds up his snifter and salutes. "Thank you, Iris, for your assistance this afternoon. Thank you, Mother . . . and a special thanks to you, Henry!"

We gaze out the window without talking. The dust finally

rests after its breathtakingly busy day. I look at Mrs. Nesbitt. Her lipstick and rouge have faded, but her eyes are as bright as the stars popping through the night sky.

I run my finger back and forth through the candle flame. A train whistles on its nighttime trip to the horizon. Mrs. Nesbitt cocks her head. The whistle moans again. She tilts her face heavenward and smiles. "That's the hobo's angel saying, '*thank yoooooou* . . . for adopting my pup.'"

CHAPTER 5

Marie cries in Dr. Nesbitt's office. Neither of us can sleep, for the same reason. We aren't *home*.

Marie's clean blanket must smell funny to her, and I'm moving like a mummy in this corset of a bed. I can't turn over. I can barely breathe.

I worm my way out, light the kerosene lantern, and kneel to examine the bedclothes. Dr. Nesbitt must have made this bed, the way the sheets and blanket are wrapped and tucked like a bandage for someone with a broken back.

Moths drawn to my lamp cast huge, fluttery shadows on the wallpaper. It is printed with barefoot goddesses floating around in togas and laurel wreaths. It is truly the strangest wallpaper I have ever seen. But the moths seem right at home in ancient Greece.

I need Hercules to unmake my bed! I yank the blanket and top sheet loose, wide awake now. I hear Marie whimpering and yowling, then footsteps and Dr. Nesbitt's soothing voice.

So far, except for helping with the ether, I am useless here. Dr. Nesbitt has done everything I was hired to do. He did the dinner dishes, pulled the shades, pumped water for us to wash our teeth, and helped his mother get ready for bed. Maybe I'm supposed to hop up and just know what to do, but I don't. They don't need me. They'll realize it soon enough.

I pull Rosie from my trunk and rub her lumpy paw over my lip. Right after Mama died I remember thinking how brave it was of Mrs. Andrews, our housekeeper even then, to take Mama's blue velvet dress without asking Daddy and turn it into a cat. She filled her with stuffing and rose sachets. I named her Rosie and I tried to connect the scent to Mama, but it wasn't true. Mama's true smell got sucked away in the sanatorium.

My trunk is bigger than the dresser. I'll never find places for everything I brought. The top drawer is already full of the necessities Mrs. Nesbitt got for me—safety matches, Pompeian Beauty Powder, a fountain pen, stamps, and . . . stationery.

Stationery . . .

I twirl my hair. My stomach drops.

I should write Daddy.

I fill the fountain pen, position a sheet of stationery on the trunk, and write the date on my first ever letter to him.

June 1, 1926
Dear Daddy,

The words are a cramped black smudge. My handwriting goes uphill, but worse is that "Dear" and "Daddy" aren't right together.

On another sheet I scratch:

Dear Father,

I still don't like "Dear," but "Father" is okay. "Father" will fit better in the post office box in Kansas City he traded for our home.

Now what? The paper is huge and endlessly blank. I write:

Thought you'd like to know I made it safely to Wellsford.
Dr. Nesbitt and his mother have an interesting house out in the country. It is a farm, but a man named Cecil Deets does the field work.

We had pineapple upside-down cake for dessert tonight. Mrs. Nesbitt has stopped using her wheelchair, but no one will say why.

I stop, add a few more lines, stop again. This is stupid. *I* sound like a bull manure salesman. It feels like lying even though it's true. It's too . . . *what*? Friendly? Daughterly? Forgiving? I watch the moths flitter around the Grecian ruins. I picture my room at home—a pitch-black box with the ceiling for a lid. That's the house of ghosts now, not this one.

A moth grazes my cheek. My letter falls facedown on the floor. When I pick it up, a tear drops right on "Dear Father," turning it into a pale puddle. I wipe my face on the bath towel folded over my footboard, take another paper, and write:

Dear Father,

I made it to Wellsford.
Dr. Nesbitt's house is a farm.
Your daughter,

Iris

I imagine my letter's trip from the mailbox at the end of the driveway, to a train, to a truck, and into Daddy's hand.

He'll read it in one gulp, hand it to Celeste. I hope they turn it over and over, looking for more. I hope he notices how much it *doesn't* say. I can see Celeste, with lipstick smeared on her front tooth, gushing, "Oh, Charles, what a fabulous idea you had hiring Iris out, she sounds so happy!"

I put out the light, crawl back in bed, and stare out into endless farm fields washed in moonlight—feeling like no more than a speck in the middle of God's dirty thumbprint.

"Avery, Marie requests a bath later this afternoon," Mrs. Nesbitt says to her son at breakfast.

Marie gnaws a crust of toast under the kitchen table. Her fur is a dull, gritty mat, shaved bare in spots from her afternoon in the operating room.

Dr. Nesbitt glances at Henry hooked to the back of his mother's chair, then back at her. "Oh, so now you're Marie's spokeswoman, her handmaiden," he replies. He rubs his eyes and stretches. "Believe me, Mother, no one knows better than I the dismal status of Miss Marie's toilette. I inhaled it all night. My diagnosis? A tawdry life of bathing in dry creek beds and stagnant swamps."

We assess Marie. She assesses us right back. Her stray eye, which I had not noticed until now, makes it hard to look her in the face. She raises her leg to scratch her torn ear, but yelps and sinks to the floor.

Dr. Nesbitt rolls his eyes. "A bath can only improve so much, Mother." He cracks her poached egg and spreads plum jam on her toast.

"I'll do it," I hear myself say.

Mrs. Nesbitt turns to me. "Iris?"

"I'll give her a bath." My offer sounds even more incredible the second time.

"Why, dear, that would be lovely. Do you have a dog at home?"

"No, ma'am. I just . . ." My hands get clammy. Why did I say that? I have no idea how to wash a dog.

"After wrestling with Marie, *you'll* need a bath too, Iris!" Dr. Nesbitt remarks.

The fact that he used "bath" and "Iris" in the same sentence is so utterly embarrassing I could die. I stare at a pool of cold egg yolk. How could he say it without *picturing* it? "I . . . I didn't mean I wanted a . . . I mean, *I* don't need a bath, I mean, I probably *do* need a bath, but . . ."

Marie whines for more toast. We've switched places, I think—the smelly dog is so at home in here. I'm the one who should crawl out the door.

Dr. Nesbitt stands, clears his throat. "Thank you, Miss Baldwin. There's a tub in the garage." He says this with a tone of doctorly authority. I think he's sorry he embarrassed me.

Outdoors, Dr. Nesbitt and I situate the tub near the windmill pump. "Keep a close eye on Mother, Iris. Until yesterday, I hadn't seen her out of that wheelchair in . . . She's been so . . ." He looks away. I sense a painful scene in his mind's eye, maybe more than one. He turns to me. "Don't say a word about her wheelchair. Might break the spell."

After breakfast, when Dr. Nesbitt goes to his office in Wellsford, Mrs. Nesbitt invites me to her room to water her plants and dust.

She seems lost in her thoughts as she taps down the hall, her hair a fine gray stream flowing over the satin collar on her robe. In her room, she strikes a theatrical pose against apricot-colored wallpaper covered with jungle flowers. The room smells of jasmine perfume and mothballs.

I know I should say something—compliment the elaborate decor, or ask just the right questions while I'm watering her violets and dusting her collection of seashells. But I feel as misplaced as Cecil Deets would be in this leafy habitat of hers.

I try to be quick and efficient with my first official housekeeping chore. I make her bed easily enough. If I barely wave the feather duster over her things I have less possibility of breaking them. I swipe her mahogany headboard—a gorgeous carved swan, so graceful it could glide right out the window. I try to ignore Mrs. Nesbitt's wheelchair, parked at the foot of her bed, with a worn-down pillow in the seat and a terrycloth bag attached to the armrest.

I dust silver frames on her nightstand with photos of men in uniform—her son, maybe, or Mr. Nesbitt—and then move along to an intricate pagoda on an ebony stand that spins.

Seated on her vanity chair, she watches my every move. I cannot wait to be finished. I turn to her. "Mrs. Nesbitt, I meant to thank you for the stationery and all. It was so nice. I already have a letter to post."

"You're very welcome. We've not had a houseguest, except Marsden, in so very long."

A guest?

In no time I've gone over everything—perfume atomizers, a porcelain hatpin holder, even her gold slippers. She sighs, a sound more exasperated than satisfied. I lower the duster. Something's wrong.

She looks out the window. I fear she's blinking back tears. What?

What?

She won't look at me. She dabs her eyes with a hankie. Should I clean her glasses? Get on the next train? I just stand there—a feather duster in one hand, a flannel rag in the other.

After a terribly long moment she asks, "Iris, your mother has passed, hasn't she?"

I look down. "Yes."

"I'd love to see her picture. Did you look alike?"

"I didn't bring one. I . . ."

She gives me a glance. "Brothers? Sisters?"

"No, ma'am."

"Your father?"

"He's gone . . . I mean, off . . . to Kansas City, and I . . ." *I wouldn't think of bringing a picture of him.*

I look at the clutter around us, wondering why, if she hates dust, she has so much stuff to collect it. She sits, head bowed, when without warning these words come out of my mouth: "Mrs. Nesbitt, would you like me to dust . . . again?"

She nods, her bent hands crumpled in her lap. "Yes. Please."

I raise the window shade. I carefully shake out the dust cloth and move it like a snail over everything I have already dusted. I polish her tortoiseshell hand mirror. I hold glass figurines for her inspection. "My husband's mother gave those to me," she says. "I never liked them, but I do now." I tilt the photos to the light for her. She doesn't want to hold them. "My hands are too lame. But please arrange them in a circle so we're all facing each other."

One by one, my hands and the rag cherish her things for her.

After a while she says, "I find that dusting brings out memories, Iris, the way rubbing a magic lamp releases the genie."

I nod to be polite, but . . . but what if your genies are asleep, or dead? What if your memories never had a chance to get made?

"My mother has passed on too." Mrs. Nesbitt looks heavenward, her eyes glistening. "We'll need to dust together every day."

"I'm bigger than you, Marie, and smarter, so get in here."

"You forgot to mention that Marie's teeth are bigger than yours," Mrs. Nesbitt says. We're behind the house. She sits on an overturned bucket, wearing a yellow sunhat, waving off the flies with a fan. There's not another house in sight, just a skinny, lone telephone line linking us to the neighbors, wherever they are. I hear bugs and the drone of a tractor. I shudder, picturing fat, greasy Cecil sitting on it.

I hoist Marie into a giant tub full of soapy water.

She yips, but thankfully doesn't scramble to get out. With one dog paddle, she's out of my reach. I kneel with one knee on an anthill and the other in the mud. The strap of my smock slips off. Flies find us, because Marie, even underwater, smells like a pile of horse manure.

Mrs. Nesbitt and I decide Marie needs a long soak before any scrubbing. The thought of accidentally touching her bare stitches or her tail stub is disgusting. So is the muck already floating in the water. She seems perfectly happy to let us pamper her.

With bread and breakfast scraps as an incentive, she splatters us through two grubby washes and a rinse which Mrs. Nesbitt insists we scent with perfume. Wet, Marie looks like a drowned river rat, but she trots around like Venus before settling into a sunny puddle of driveway dirt.

I dump out the tub. My smock and hair are soaked. I've got grit under my fingernails and dog hair in my mouth. "I take that back about who's smarter," I tell Mrs. Nesbitt. "I'm the wet dog and she smells like jasmine."

CHAPTER 6

June 2, 1926
Dear Leroy,

I have been in Wellsford for one
whole night and day. This is what I have
accomplished so far:
killed a bum
amputated a dog's tail
drank brandy
took an eye test

and ate a peppermint.

Ha!

If you want details, write back.

Please tell Carl I donated my reverse-leather suede boots to the Burlington Railroad.

Say hello to Mrs. Andrews.

How's your new ice delivery job?

Have you started to miss me?

Your friend,

Iris Louise Baldwin

(Who you plan to come visit very soon.)

P.S. They keep a shotgun by the kitchen door. I wonder if it's loaded.

Blood is everywhere—the sheets, the ticking, even my pillowcase!

I've stuffed a bath towel between my legs, so now I'm ruining it, too. The only other choice is Mrs. Nesbitt's hankie.

"When *it* happens, keep it to yourself," Mrs. Andrews had warned when she explained menstruation to me last year. The conversation lasted less than a minute, with no time for questions. "It's a nasty medical condition, a curse on women. Do your utmost to guard against leakage, odor, accidents . . ."

So far, I have failed. How can I keep *this* a secret?

I turn on my side, stare out the window. Shifty wind brushes the corn rows—green then silver then green again.

There's a war in my stomach, or is it my back, or both? I would like to die.

For the last two years I've worried about *it* to death—that I'd start in the middle of Latin or physical education. Then I feared it wouldn't ever happen. But why didn't I think it could start here? How could I have packed my whole trunk and brought nothing—no rags or pads?

Outside our shoe store window I used to watch ladies, some of them mothers of girls in my class, go into Lowen's Pharmacy and come out with a bulky sack—their "silent purchase." The store had a system—you put money in a box and took a package of Kotex pads off the counter without saying anything to anybody. I was so dumb not to do that. My stupidity doesn't go in a cycle. I'm stupid all the time.

Dr. Nesbitt's got an office full of gauze bandages and clean rags, maybe even a stack of diapers somewhere. But I can't sneak in there . . . stupid, *stupid.* His office is so tidy, he'd notice if I borrowed a safety pin.

I rearrange the towel. From the kitchen come Dr. and Mrs. Nesbitt's voices and the clink of teaspoons. I smell coffee and toast. Dr. Nesbitt is cooking breakfast. Then he'll do the rest of my jobs before he goes to work.

I'm trapped. Even if I pretend I'm sick, they'll see the ruined towel and *know*. If I had three wishes in the world, they would all be for a box of Kotex and two safety pins.

Oh, God . . . here comes Marie. Her toenails *clickity-click* on the strips of hardwood beside the carpet runner. She bumps my door open and looks at me cockeyed. I can see sunlight through the tear in her ear, but she's definitely fluffier now, almost shiny. I sniff her jasmine perfume.

She puts her front paws on the mattress and sniffs me. "Ugh. For God's sake, Marie, git. Go get some toast." I flap my hands. "Shoo!"

But she just sniffs more. She does some doggy circles like she's contemplating what to do next. I swear she seems to be thinking.

She trots outside the dining room door and barks.

"Shut up, Marie. Bye-*bye*!"

She barks again, this time more shrilly.

Help. Please, please, don't anybody come in here.

"Scram!"

She minds me by scramming right back into the kitchen and barking her head off.

An eternity passes. The phone rings—a short and two longs. Not the Nesbitts' code. Roosters, robins, everybody is up and running but me. I hear *tap . . . tap . . . tap.*

It's Henry.

In another eternity Mrs. Nesbitt peeks in the door. I'm completely turned inside out, all smelly horribleness.

She assesses the scene in an instant. "Bottom drawer." I stare at her, uncomprehending. She nods toward the chest. "We'll do wash this afternoon instead of dusting." She leaves, shutting the door behind her.

In the bureau are three dark blue boxes with white crosses and one word printed on them: Kotex. My hands fumble trying to pin the thick pad into clean underwear. The wallpaper goddesses watch. What help are they, flying around in their see-through gowns? You don't read myths about this.

I roll my dirty clothes and pillowcase, and the stained towel inside the sheets so that not one speck of red shows, and waddle down the hall, all the while praying, *Please, God, have Dr. Nesbitt be gone by now.* I walk on the outsides of my feet. The pad feels like a bale of hay.

"He already left," Mrs. Nesbitt says with a sympathetic smile when I step into the kitchen. I set the laundry pile on the back porch and shrink into a kitchen chair. She shrugs. "A wash with bluing will take care of it. How are you feeling?"

Mrs. Nesbitt and Marie silently watch me sob into a napkin. But it's not my "time of the month" making me cry, it's their motherly help. Like magic, they turned awful to easy.

"I'd rather wash you in that tub than wash sheets in *this*," I tell Marie after breakfast. The Nesbitt's washing machine is yellow with two wooden tubs—one for washing and one for rinse. There's a wringer that'll scalp me if one hair gets caught in it. It already squished a grasshopper, leaving a smear of yellow-green on my pillowcase. Mrs.

Andrews' washer was electric. This one's got a gas engine that sputters grease.

When I'm finished the sheets aren't shredded, nor are they perfectly white, but they're close. I'm sure there are traces of grease and grasshopper guts and my time of the month if you took a magnifying glass to them.

Mrs. Nesbitt has gone inside to take a nap. Dr. Nesbitt should be back soon. There is no way he will just say hello and go in his clinic without noticing my sheets—giant banners announcing, *Hear ye, hear ye, Iris Baldwin has her period.*

Thank goodness there's a breeze. I shake the sheets and wrestle them over the clothesline. I don't hear the horse and wagon until it's all the way up our drive.

Cecil Deets.

He just sits up there on the wagon bench with a smug look. "Strange. Not their usual laundry day," he remarks, chewing a wad of tobacco. His eyes dart around, probably looking for Mrs. Nesbitt. "You look like you could use a hand."

"No," I say too sharply. "No, thank you."

He jumps off the seat, glances at me, and rubs the hem of one of my sheets between his grimy fingers. "Where's the lady of the house?"

But before I can answer, Marie leaps off the back porch and charges at Cecil, her teeth bared. She acts part wolf, part bear. Cecil kicks at her, then hops back in his wagon. "Holy shit!" He squints at her, and says, "Oh, I know *you*. You're the stinkin' mutt beggin' scraps around my place. Your dead hobo musta underfed ya."

A strip of fur down Marie's back rises. Her ears flatten.

Despite the cuts and bruises she looks ready to attach her teeth to his ankle.

"Marie, stop that," I say. But she doesn't.

"*Marie?*" Cecil makes that burpy laugh. "Huh!" He gives the sheets a good once-over, and then gives me the same. He raises his eyebrows, lowers his voice. "Yep, you're more matured than my Dot. Just how long they hired you for?" I look away without answering, desperate to hear Dr. Nesbitt's car.

The three of us are caught together for a long, awful moment.

"You ever need any kind of help around here when the doctor's gone, just let me know, Miss Iris Baldwin." He shakes his head, as though I must be confused. "It's surely a puzzle—*you* out here with the laundry instead of Dot."

Go away . . .

He spits in the dust, clucks his horse, and as slow as a slug, turns his rig around.

. . . and never come again.

"*I will not report the events of this day to Leroy* in my next letter," I tell Marie, sitting on my bed later that afternoon. She's pooped. No wonder—she's been taking care of me all day. "Yesterday I would have put you through the washing machine *and* the wringer, and today you're my new best friend." I rub her head. "What happened between you and Cecil Deets?" She looks up at me. "You know something, don't you?"

I lie back. Every part of me either aches or drips or throbs. Mrs. Nesbitt's still in bed too. She doesn't seem to feel well today, either.

I have three thoughts—a good one, a new one, and an awful one. The good one is how Mrs. Nesbitt planned for me, looked forward to my coming with the stamps and body powder and Kotex she bought.

My new thought is that I never once considered she'd be curious about me; that she'd talk, much less ask questions; that we'd have anything in common.

Now the awful thought. If Mrs. Nesbitt didn't go to town for my silent purchase, which I'm pretty sure is right, then who did? I shudder. "Oh, please let it be a catalog order," I say to Marie, "or even Dr. Nesbitt.

"Anybody but Cecil."

"Supper from Miss Olive Nish tonight," Dr. Nesbitt announces, unloading two covered containers on the kitchen counter. "The perfect trade-off for trimming her ingrown toenails—yams marinated in sorghum molasses and green beans in bacon grease."

My stomach lurches. Mrs. Nesbitt walks into the kitchen with Henry, rested and smiling. Dr. Nesbitt starts to grab her arm, then stops himself. Instead he pecks her on the cheek. After a day of toenail trimming and God knows what else, his hair still looks like he parted it with a scalpel.

"How'd you get along today?" he asks, kneeling beside Marie on the floor. He feels her ribs, parts her fur and examines her stitches and her tail. "Looks like we missed a spot on your ear, but, all in all, you look beautiful."

"And strong," I say.

Dr. Nesbitt sorts through the mail. Marie sighs—a long, satisfied sound—and falls asleep. Mrs. Nesbitt suggests we plant marigold seeds by the front stoop. I don't mention Cecil or the cranky washing machine. I just listen to a soft summer rain drum the back porch roof.

CHAPTER 7

I've lost track of the days. Sunday slipped into Monday before I caught hold of it.

"We used to go," is all Mrs. Nesbitt has said about church.

But this morning we've got the *very reverent* Dorothy "Dot" Deets here instead of a minister.

"I knew you were at the Nesbitts now, but who cares? Their laundry is *my* job," she hisses, sizing me up the moment I step out into the yard. She stands, hands on her hips. "Your kin as gangly as you?" She's short and roly-poly like her name, with springy red hair and chapped cheeks. She wears a sack dress and worn out lace-up boots. She's like girls at school who let the catty comments in their heads exit right out of their mouths. "So are you just gonna stand there starin' or what?" She bugs her eyes at me. "I ain't wantin' your help."

I had been watching her from the kitchen window, and what she really means is, *I ain't needin' your help snooping through the Nesbitts' laundry.*

But something tells me to just keep *starin'* while Dot digs through the dirty clothes. After a minute I ask casually, "So, what're you finding in that basket?"

Dot scowls. "Where you come from?"

"Atchison." I know she's trying to piece together where I fit with her and why there's none of my laundry in the basket. "Where do *you* live, Dot?"

"A mile that way," she points with her head, then returns to her digging and sniffing. I guess she's decided to continue the laundry investigation with me watching. She holds one of Mrs. Nesbitt's hankies to the light, smells it, and frowns. "Why's the old woman wearing perfume all the sudden? And look . . ." She glances toward the house, then shoves the hankie toward me. "It'll take all day to get this damn lipstick out. Most folks I have the acquaintance of think she's a"—Dot pinches her nose—"*snob*. But I say more like a witch . . . the way she just gave up her wheelchair and started walking." Dot snaps her chubby fingers. "How can somebody do that? You're either lame or you ain't."

"When was that, that she started walking?"

"A few weeks ago. I saw her practicing back and forth on the porch with a cane. She's plain strange."

Dot plucks out a dinner napkin and sniffs a stain. Her

eyes light up. "Whiskey!" She waves it like a white flag. "Here, smell. Imagine him doctorin' people with a gut full of moonshine."

"How do you know what whiskey smells like?"

Her voice is hushed. "All I know is that Dr. Nesbitt keeps liquor in the dining room closet in a fancy bottle." I nod, barely stopping myself from asking exactly how she knows *that*.

Dot pokes at an ink stain on the pocket of Dr. Nesbitt's shirt. "Still writing those fancy letters." She rolls her eyes. "He's got somebody in New York City—you know," she wags her head, "corresponding back and forth every single week, but the lady never visits." Dot's eyebrows shoot up and stay there. "Because I bet she's already married to somebody else! All these folks just love Doc Nesbitt." Dot sniffs. She's clearly not a passenger on *that* ship of fools. "But one thing he can't do is count. He pays me per piece, never checks my numbers. My daddy don't understand why he's still livin' with his *mama*." She scrubs a spot of Marie's blood with a brick of lye soap. "Where's your things?" she asks, reaching the bottom of the load.

"I do my own."

She curls her lip. This tidbit will fuel theories about the snotty, too-good-for-regular-country-washing girl the Nesbitts hired. "You like 'em?" she asks.

"Who?"

"Who you think I mean? Miz Nesbitt and him."

Marie hops off the porch, sending chickens onto the driveway. She tilts her nose, walks past Dot, and whines at me. "Looks like Mrs. Nesbitt needs something," I say. Dot's eyes darken. I walk inside and sit at the kitchen table with Mrs. Nesbitt, who is figuring her crossword puzzle. Next to it is a postcard. She slides it over to me, message-side down. It's from Leroy.

June 5

Iris,

How are you?

I am writing this at our spot.

It has been 99 $\frac{3}{4}$ hours since you left.

Wellsford sounds real interesting, especially the dead hobo and the eye test. Did you pass it?

Atchison is buggy.

My ice job is either too hot or too cold.

Warmly (!)

LP

I smile at Mrs. Nesbitt, put the card in my pocket. I can't help but wonder if she has already read it.

"What's a word for halo, Iris—six letters, starts with 'n'?" she says, pointing to the puzzle.

I think a moment. "Try 'nimbus.' I remember the word from Sunday School." She nods. I write the letters in the squares for her.

"How about an 'r' word for embarrassed. Eight letters, hyphenated."

"Uh . . . hmmm . . . Give me a minute."

Mrs. Nesbitt holds up her hand. "Don't worry. We'll think of it."

I take our kerosene globes out on the back porch to scrub with Dot's old wash water while she hangs the laundry. The wet soot runs down my arms. I grip the glass. I do not want to break one in front of her. "I can take the clothes off later," I say, "if you want to go on." I study the clotheslines. "How many pieces today, Dot?"

"Thirty-eight," she says, the way someone might say *shut up*.

Dot waltzes past me and pops her head in the back door. "Forgive me for interrupting your puzzle, Miz Nesbitt, but you need Borax Powder, ma'am. Oh, and I told Iris that it is a pure pleasure washing such fine things as you and Dr. Nesbitt own. It'll be thirty-eight pieces today, ma'am, and thank you."

"Thank you. I'll inform Avery."

I watch Dot flounce off down the driveway, her hair blazing like a lit tumbleweed.

I dry the globes, then go in and sit with Mrs. Nesbitt. We study the crossword from an old edition of *The Kansas City Star* newspaper. "How's Dot?" she asks.

"I told her I'd take the wash down, so she could go on

home. She didn't look happy, but she left." I don't tell Mrs. Nesbitt that Dot uses a bushel barrel too much soap in the tub, or that she charged for thirty-eight when it was only thirty-five, or that she *reads* our laundry like a diary. "How long has she been doing the wash?"

Mrs. Nesbitt shifts in her chair. A shadow crosses her face. "Since her mother, Pansy, left. Not quite a year."

I look up from the crossword. "Pansy Deets *left*? Cecil told me his wife passed on."

Mrs. Nesbitt nods. "You'd better make us some tea."

I light the stove and fill the kettle.

"Dot also claims her mother passed on, but she didn't. She's not dead." Mrs. Nesbitt drops silent. Sets her mouth.

I put tea bags in our cups and wait for the water to boil. It's so quiet, it seems even the chickens are listening. Marie curls up at Mrs. Nesbitt's feet.

She shakes her head. "When Avery and I moved here seven years ago, I was in an awful way."

I look over at her. "Ma'am?"

"Melancholia. That's why we came—Avery thought it might help me. This was my other son, Morris's, farm. We moved after he was killed. Avery leased the land to tenants and we kept the house. His widow didn't want it." She looks up. I wonder if she's picturing his widow's face. Water *drip*, *drip*s in the catch pan under the icebox. Tears begin to drain down the creases in Mrs. Nesbitt's cheeks. She covers her face, bows her head, and sobs.

The teapot pings and creaks on the burner. I've never seen an old person cry like this. The sadness from life is supposed to be folded inside an old person, not streaming out. I trace the wood grain pattern on the table with my fingertip, feeling helpless, hopeless to know what to do. My eyes start to burn and now I'm crying too, over I don't even know what. After a moment Mrs. Nesbitt slides her hankie to me.

The kettle whistles. We look up at each other. Mrs. Nesbitt smiles sadly. I wipe her glasses, wondering how many times she's had to recover from feeling bad—hundreds of times more than me.

She pats stray hairs back into her bun, clears her throat. "Avery established his medical practice and got busy with his office out here and his clinic in town. I was in particular need of company when Pansy happened along, ready to do housekeeping and cooking. Despite our age difference, I could tell we both had hollow spots inside." Mrs. Nesbitt suddenly looks up at me—right through me really, and nods as though she knows I have those very same holes in me. "Anyway, I knew the reasons for mine, but Pansy was tight-lipped. She was full of steam with no vent."

"Steam?"

"Fury at her husband, at herself. She lacked backbone. I think Cecil had bruised it one time too many."

"You mean he hit her?"

"Like I said, she was tight-lipped. Stoic . . . or maybe paralyzed in fear. I saw the marks." Mrs. Nesbitt brushes her fingertips over a spot below her ear. "Pansy didn't try to cover them up—I guess she let her bruises speak for themselves. But she wouldn't allow Avery to examine her, even when I'm sure she had broken ribs."

I pour the water. Steam releases around us.

"I knew things were getting worse with Cecil. One afternoon last fall she announced she wanted to take Dot and go to her sister's."

Mrs. Nesbitt grips the edge of the table. Her hands look tiny and withered. "I was all for it. Gave her money for their train fare."

Marie sighs in her sleep. Dr. Nesbitt's night shirts wave at us from the clothesline.

"By dawn Pansy was gone. She had walked the four miles to the depot, bought a one-way ticket to Chicago, and there's been no trace of her since."

I hold my cup with both hands, imagining Pansy trudging alone in the dark.

"Cecil didn't say a word. He just referred to Pansy as '*passed on*,' which is partly correct I guess."

"So Cecil doesn't know about your talks with Pansy or the money?"

"I'm sure he suspects it. Pansy didn't have a penny to her name, or so she said. She told me he took everything she made."

"But how could she just leave Dot?"

"Maybe a trade for her freedom—Dot was always 'daddy's special girl.' Pansy's heart was just one big bruise, not working right."

"Maybe Dot refused to go."

Mrs. Nesbitt lifts her cup, takes a sip. "Maybe."

Mrs. Nesbitt glances out at the clothesline. "That's when I hired Dot to do the laundry—so she'd have some income and, I don't know, maybe I could keep an eye on her some-how. But she's shifty like her daddy, and closed-mouthed like her mama." Mrs. Nesbitt shakes her head. "I was stu-pid to get involved with them. I needed somebody to need me. But a wise person would have stayed away. A wise per-son wouldn't believe a word they say."

I stand on a chair by the clothesline, furious that Pansy used Mrs. Nesbitt, lied right in her face, and left her daughter in Cecil's hands. I see Dot's curled lip and her ruddy cheeks.

Red-faced.

That's it!

"Red-faced!" I yell, jumping off the chair. "The cross-word for embarrassed is 'red-faced,'" I say, running in the kitchen door.

Mrs. Nesbitt claps. "Ah, yes! Thank you, dear."

I write the word on the squares, then stand a moment, weighing whether to say the next thing that has popped into my head. I don't. But I have figured the perfect eight letter word, *hyphenated*, to describe Dot and her mother.

Two-faced!

But then, Dot must need a hundred faces to survive liv-ing alone with Cecil. I felt two-faced the instant I met him—trying to mind my manners, trying to act polite to the devil.

CHAPTER 8

June 14, 1926
Dear Iris,

Thank you for your letter.
We have been so busy, it is impossible to
believe two weeks have passed. Getting
the store in order requires long hours,
meetings with my investors, contracts
with vendors, and countless design
decisions. It leaves little time to write.

I thought of you this morning when I heard from Carl. He says the Atchison store is practically running itself! He hired Constance Dithers and her daughter, Faith, to work out front. I plan a trip to Atchison in late July to check the books and oversee the shoe orders for fall.

We must finalize the name for the Kansas City store and get our sign painter to work. One can't start advertising too soon. Here are the choices:

Baldwin's Bootery
A step ahead

Uptown Shoes
Shake off that cow town dust, put on our uptown shoes.

What's your vote? Mine is Baldwin's Bootery. Celeste likes the uptown theme. Our painter charges by the letter, so a long slogan is pricey. But image is everything! We're surrounded by upscale establishments. Window shoppers need an inducement to come in and spend!

Thank goodness Celeste is an absolute wizard with window dressing!

Kansas City is truly "on the move" with boulevards, baseball, mansions, Petticoat Lane, and a magnificent railway station. There is even an airfield. Next thing you know I'll buy a plane and take flying lessons! Until then, I have bought a new Cadillac with a V-8 engine. It is a dream to drive and will cut down my travel time between stores. Celeste says the upholstery is "heaven." What make does Dr. Nesbitt drive?

Now for the big news. Celeste and I are engaged. We selected a ring at Jaccard's Jewelry last week. It is being fitted. By the time you receive this, it will be official. She has informed her family, and by this correspondence, I have informed mine. You are free to spread the news. So be happy for us.

Give my regards to the doctor and his mother. I know they are grateful to have you.

Love,
Daddy

P.S.
Dear Iris,

My engagement to your father is a dream come true! I know the news may take some getting used to. I can't wait for you to see the ring and celebrate with us.

Did you know they call Kansas City the "Paris of the Plains"? It's the fountains and the fashion! You simply must see it!!!

Au revoir!
Celeste

I sit on the floor with my back against the bed frame, and read the letter out loud to Marie. When I finish, she scratches her head and looks at me cross-eyed. "My feelings exactly." I wave the letter at her. "Six exclamation points in the P.S.! They're like thumbtacks holding her *dreamy* news on the paper. It sounds like they're trying to sell me something.

"Maybe Celeste helped him write it. Or maybe that's how he acts all the time now, happily away from Atchison and from me." I rub Marie's ears. "I know why he asked about Dr. Nesbitt's car . . . just scratching up something to say before the big headline. If they hadn't gotten engaged, I wouldn't have heard from him." Marie yawns. "What's your vote on the name? I don't like either of them. The one with two 'uptowns' is so long nobody will be able to see the shoes. Any window whiz should know that."

Daddy's phony letter is full of places where he could have left the "Paris of the Plains" topic and asked about me. I know why he didn't. If my answer isn't full of cheery exclamation points, he won't know what to do, except ignore it.

I swipe my sleeve across my forehead, lift my hair off my shoulders. Marie watches me fold the letter back in its envelope and stuff it in my Kotex drawer.

"There," I tell her, "now I won't have to think about Daddy and Celeste for a whole month!"

I stare at the wallpaper goddesses. "How'd you do it? Your fathers were worse than mine. They double-crossed you, traded you, sacrificed you, and you still flutter around all fresh in your gauzy gowns like everything's perfect. I guess if you live forever you learn to get over, and over, and over things. You either float on . . . or get revenge."

Marie yawns and thumps her stumpy tail on the floor. I blot my neck with a hankie.

What now?

I go to the kitchen for a drink of water. Instead, without the slightest plan to do so, I fill two big pitchers and carry them to my room. I fix a bowl with water for Marie and the wash basin for me. I lock the door, pull the shades, take off my shoes and socks, my damp dress, and all my under things. The goddesses watch me lather my washcloth and clean every part of me—my face, my breasts, between my toes, the small of my back, my throat. A breeze ruffles Marie's fur, hits my wet skin. I stand shivering with my arms draped like wings and drip dry.

After a sprinkle of Pompeian Beauty Powder, I step into my favorite cotton dress that's white with yellow flowers and lacy sleeves. I twist my hair into a knot and wash my teeth. When I open the shades, the sun creates stepping stones of light on the rug. I walk across them to the buffet mirror and pinch my cheeks. There. I've washed off that Kansas City dust and put on my goddess shoes.

I float out of the dining room . . . barefoot.

Mrs. Nesbitt's eyes light up when she sees me. "You look like a fresh bouquet on this wilted afternoon." She looks at my feet and smiles, then inhales, tilts her head back. "I love the scent of your powder."

"Thank you."

"I saw you received a letter from your father. How is his new store in Kansas City coming along?"

I shrug. "Okay."

My voice sounds anything but okay. I turn, straighten the stack of folded crossword puzzles, and clear the dish rack. I do not look at Mrs. Nesbitt, but I feel her eyes on me.

After a moment she says, "Henry needs exercise. Let's check the roses and water our marigolds."

I get garden gloves, a bucket full of coffee grounds and crushed eggshells, and the watering can off the back porch.

Mrs. Nesbitt sits on the shady front steps. We are surrounded by hundreds of sprouts. "It's hard to tell the weeds from the flowers," I say.

"Let's treat them all the same until we know for sure."

I shake a little compost over the seedlings, then barely tip the sprinkling can for fear I'll wash them right out of the dirt.

"They're hardier than they seem," Mrs. Nesbitt remarks.

We walk to a huge elm in the front yard that has an old spring wagon seat on a frame under it. We are surrounded by a brilliant green lawn. Mrs. Nesbitt props Henry against the trunk, steps out of her slippers, and pats the plank seat. "Morris made this."

I drain the watering can into a little stone birdbath.

"If you don't mind, let's sit together awhile," she says.

Wavy heat rises around us, but under the tree it's surprisingly pleasant. "Our house looks interesting from this point of view, don't you think? It's revealing to look *at* it, rather than *from* it." Mrs. Nesbitt waves her Japanese fan. "Inside it's . . . *divided*—all walls and doors—but this way it looks whole and sturdy. I should come out here every day."

Leaf patterns swim across the pale gray stucco. The storm cellar door is choked shut by roots—Mother Nature's lock. I think how easily, how kindly they have folded me into their house.

Dr. Nesbitt's office, with its outside entrance, looks added on. We talk about the patients who have come there the past few weeks—the screaming six-year-old boy who had stepped on a fishhook. I tell how I tried to keep his mother calm while Dr. Nesbitt pushed the hook through and cut off the barb. Or the night a man and his wife showed up. He claimed she had "turned into a mannequin," wouldn't move—a "possession by Satan." She sat on the passenger seat unblinking while the husband poured his frustration out on us. "Your wife needs help at the state hospital," Dr. Nesbitt had said as kindly as any human could.

I study the long front-room windows. She has yet to suggest we clean the parlor, even though it's caked with dust. I've never seen Dr. Nesbitt's bedroom, but knowing him, he scours it before he goes to bed every night.

"The house is really filling up," Mrs. Nesbitt says. "Avery and me, you, Marie, Henry."

"Don't forget my wallpaper goddesses."

Mrs. Nesbitt claps. "Yes! That's what I mean. The house is filling up!"

The windmill squeaks. A woodpecker *rat-a-tat-tat*s against

the garage shingles. Without warning four words march out of my mouth. "My father is engaged."

We watch a blue jay swoop the birdbath, bully a wet sparrow into the elm. I hop up. "Shoo! Shoo!"

"That's important news, Iris."

"I guess. Her name's Celeste." So much for my month of silence.

"When will they marry?" she asks softly.

"He didn't say."

For some reason Mama pops into my head. I imagine her here with us, listening and shaking her head for poor, unsuspecting Celeste. But why do I think she'd do that? What if Mama was actually *just like* Celeste, or any of Daddy's other girlfriends? I have no way of knowing. I squash that black thought.

"Do you know Celeste well?"

"Celeste? No!" I can only imagine what Mrs. Nesbitt must be thinking of me. *My, Iris certainly sounds stand-offish. She should be happy for her father. What has she done to have such a poor relationship with him?*

And that is one thing I truly have no answer for—what have I done or not done?

Mrs. Nesbitt gazes at me a long moment. "Then Celeste must not know you very well either."

Crows fuss at each other on our phone wire.

"What's your father like, dear?"

"Uh . . . he drives too fast . . . he hates coughing because it sounds like tuberculosis, and he hates cheap shoes, and . . ." It sounds like trivial nothing. My heart twists on itself. I need another goddess bath. "He never talks about himself, so I . . ."

"Do you take after your father, Iris?"

"No!"

She covers my hand with hers. "Do you take after your mother, then?"

"Oh, yes," I lie, staring in my lap. "Yes, I do."

That night in bed, my thoughts dart and bump like sparrows flown down the chimney.

I try to move Celeste easily and kindly into our Atchison house, but I get only as far as the porch swing. The thought of her acting lovey-dovey with my father on the divan is horrible. So are her knickknacks, her powerful perfume, her giggle. How can she like him?

There's no moon tonight. The room is so dark, I can't tell if my eyes are open or not, but I can see Celeste bringing Daddy sugar cubes for his coffee, straightening his collar, hanging new pictures, moving our furniture.

I can't recall Mama's laugh or her saying "I love you," or "Change your socks," or "Let's play jacks." Nothing. Daddy closed her memory with her coffin. I don't remember anything we did together except blink-talk. I have only one or two of Mama's things hibernating in that house until I get back in September. And now here comes Celeste to rearrange them.

And what, I wonder, am I supposed to call her when she's sitting all dolled up and perky at the breakfast table after spending the night in my father's bedroom?

"Do I just say, oh, *good morning*, Mother?"

Nope.

She is not the mother type. She is not *my* type, no matter what I call her.

I repeat "Mother." Just a pop of my lips, a thrust of my tongue, and there it is—a perfect little pair of syllables hanging together in the air. "Mother." The voice belongs to me, but the word doesn't. It belongs to everybody *but* me. "Mother" slides out of Dr. Nesbitt's mouth as easily as "please" and "thank you."

I practice it a few times—softly, like the little girl on the train with her play-act family.

I tilt it up in a question. "Mother?"

I stamp it sternly on the air. "Mother!"

I singsong it. "Mo-ther."

I whisper it out the window, yell it in my pillow, float it like smoke.

"Mo . . . ther . . . mo . . . ther . . . mo . . . ther . . . moth . . ."

I pour it out to the black night, until finally, the syllables get tired and fall apart.

CHAPTER 9

"What make of car do you drive, Dr. Nesbitt?"
I ask at breakfast early Saturday morning. I feel dumb. All
I know is that his automobile is black, but that won't answer
my father's question.

"Ford Model T Tudor Sedan." Dr. Nesbitt mops up the
yolk of his poached egg with a piece of toast. "Do you drive?"

"Me? Oh no, sir." I cut the stems and put three straw-
berries on Mrs. Nesbitt's plate.

A breeze ruffles the curtains. Dr. Nesbitt glances out.
"Looks clear today. After I do the lawn, I'll teach you." He
rinses his plate in the sink, gives his mother and me a nod,
and heads out to the garage for the mower.

Mrs. Nesbitt looks at me, surprised. She shakes her head in a phony lament. "Oh, boy, a whole afternoon spent stirring up the roads. We'll be dusting for weeks!"

I picture myself spinning dirt devils out of the exhaust pipe. I smile, but truly, I'd rather be dusting than driving. You can't kill anybody with a dustcloth.

By lunchtime my stomach is a knot.

In the driveway Dr. Nesbitt insists I sit in the driver's seat. "We will begin," he says in a serious way, "with the three easiest driving skills to master. Number one: stalling the engine. Number two: getting stuck in a ditch. And number three: getting lost." He looks at me without cracking a grin. "Which'll it be?"

"How about going backward when you mean to go forward," I say with a laugh that sounds more than slightly hysterical.

The seat is hard and high. For the first time in my life I'm glad to be gangly. We review the foot pedals: gears on the left, reverse in the middle, and engine brake on the right. "Driving is much easier for folks with three legs," Dr. Nesbitt remarks. We review the two levers on either side of the steering wheel and the two on the floor. "And four arms."

After a string of directions, I start the engine. The car jumps to life. I inhale so sharply I choke. I am petrified. What's a "Tudor Sedan" anyway? A booby trap? Over the engine noise Dr. Nesbitt says to press the left pedal to the floor for low gear. Next he says to adjust the throttle. *Throttle?* My hands flutter up and down. *Throttle . . . throttle . . .* I spot it! *Okay.* I move the right steering wheel lever to "*give her a little gas*." Mrs. Nesbitt waves Henry at us from the back porch. Our tires spray gravel. "Get out of the way," I scream at the chickens as we buck forward.

"Now brake," Dr. Nesbitt says, calm as can be.

I press the right pedal. We stall out. I exhale for what seems like the first time in hours. Panting, I turn to Dr. Nesbitt with my mouth hanging open.

"Well done, Iris. You mastered skill number one on the first try."

I learn neutral and reverse and quite a bit about horsepower and flat tires and electric starters versus the old crank style. Dr. Nesbitt tells how he used to treat drivers with a "Ford Fracture"—the broken arm they got when a crank starter accidentally spun the wrong way.

I've sweated through my dress again. My shoulders ache from being hunched to my ears. My fingers won't release from the steering wheel. Mrs. Nesbitt watches from the porch, smiling and waving like we are her children going round and round on a carnival ride. Poor Marie is pooped. She's worn a strip in the grass trying to chase us.

I turn off the ignition and mop my forehead. I have been driving now for almost two hours and we haven't left the driveway.

"At least we didn't get lost," I say.

Dr. Nesbitt smiles. "You seem like a natural, Iris, truly. In a few days you'll have this car climbing telephone poles."

I get out and slam the door. "Yes, sir . . . in reverse."

June 17, 1926
Dear Leroy,

Dr. Nesbitt is teaching me to drive! It's actually fun. Maybe I take after Daddy a little—but not his reckless, show-off style.

Driving is lots easier than cooking, which is something I can't steer away from any longer. Help! The other night when we faced another sloppy bowl of limp cucumbers floating in vinegar, Mrs. Nesbitt said, "Why can't any of the good cooks in Wellsford get sick."

With a cookbook and Mrs. Nesbitt's help I've learned biscuits, oatmeal (big deal), and creamed corn, but so far, when I'm through the kitchen mostly smells like scorched potholders.

When you visit (I think the Nesbitts would say it's okay) we'll take a chicken coop tour. I'm in charge of it now. No admission fee. Pee-yew and UGH . . . hens are crabby. I wonder if the art of cooking includes choking your own chickens?

The girl at the farm "next door" has it out for me. Her name is Dot.

Dot = hen + snapping turtle.

Her mama's gone. Dot claims she passed on, but really she ran off because her husband hit her. What's worse—having your mama disappear in the middle of the night or pass on? I say getting left high and dry is worse. Maybe that's why Dot's so mean.

Another "ugh"—Daddy is engaged to Celeste Simmons. I should have seen it coming. Everybody in Atchison already knows, right? Celeste is the opposite of Dot—too cuddly, with a giant helping of phony. Maybe she won't last, just like all his other lady friends. I swear I am not going to think about it.

Thank you for the postcard. If you don't want the chickens and everyone else in the world to read them before I do, try a letter in an envelope.

I miss you a whole lot—so there.
ILB

P.S. Please come. Chicken tour is optional.

On Sunday, while most folks are at church, I'm back in the driver's seat. Dr. Nesbitt's wearing old work pants and a straw hat. "It's time to hit the road," he says. I don't tell him how last night when I couldn't sleep I *drove* sitting on a dining room chair. The goddesses thought I was a talking octopus.

I start the car and adjust the levers and pedals. We glide down the driveway. Thankfully I avoid picking off the telephone pole and the mailbox, and then I make such a sharp left turn, I wheel us in a complete circle. As we buck and hump along I feel sure an octopus could drive better than me. "I'm sorry," I say without taking my eyes from the road. "I hope I don't shake your teeth out."

Dr. Nesbitt is quiet a long moment. "Years ago, right before my father died, he taught Mother to drive. Dad insisted on it, knowing she'd have to be independent. I can still see them cruising around our old neighborhood—Morris and me cheering her from the curb. She needed a big pillow at her back so she could reach the pedals. Once you learn, Iris, I hope you two will get out." He smiles. "Do the town!"

We pass a walnut orchard and a thin dirt road leading to a white box farmhouse surrounded by trees. It seems to spin slowly to watch us go by. I steer around the Rawleigh man's yellow medicine buggy and an abandoned truck with two flat tires.

"If Mother were here, she'd insist we get out and dust it," Dr. Nesbitt remarks.

A horse and wagon lope ahead of us in the distance. My heart stops.

Okay.

Think.

Which is the brake . . . find the brake pedal and the parking brake. Just slow down a bit. Don't stall. My mind's running faster than the car. Where's the horn? Where's the *horn?*

Oh, God. It's Cecil and Dot.

They stop. I creep up and stall inches behind them. From the corner of my eye I see Dr. Nesbitt press an imaginary brake pedal on the passenger side.

Cecil nudges Dot. They swivel around on the seat to face us. "Well, well. What have we here?" I clench the steering wheel, brace for Dr. Nesbitt to put me on the spot, make some smart remarks about my driving—either a brag, *Iris is a whiz behind the wheel,* or a snide *Good thing we stalled, it's the only way Iris can stop this thing.* But the real Dr. Nesbitt looks from Dot to Cecil to me without saying a word.

I sit straighter, adjust my sleeves, and watch Dot size things up. Her eyes are wary, not piggy like her father's. I wonder if he sees Pansy every time he looks at her. Dot curls her lip ever so subtly at me, then smiles at Dr. Nesbitt. I know she's busy twisting this moment into a string of nasty remarks.

Cecil spits. "Et looks like your *horsey* stalled out on you, Miss Baldwin."

I don't answer. Cecil's mare pees in the dirt.

Dr. Nesbitt asks, "What about that old *horsey* you bought,

Cecil? Is that rusted Chevy you're always tinkering with still on the fritz?"

"You know I prefer *ree-al* horsepower," says Cecil, with what is supposed to be a charming country bumpkin tone. He squeezes Dot's knee. "I told my girl, 'A horse'll stop at a barbed-wire fence. But, I ask you, will a car?'" Cecil gets a self-satisfied expression, as though he's the first person to be born with brains. "A car will drive right off a bluff, but will a horse?" He folds his arms.

"I don't know as I can say," Dr. Nesbitt remarks. "I've never seen a horse drive a car."

"I guess we'll have to save getting lost for another day," he says as we pull up our long driveway and stop. We have churned the dust on dozens of county roads. I've learned how to stop without stalling. I no longer head straight into every ditch. I'm getting reverse, and I even wormed around a Sunday driver who was pokier than me.

Dr. Nesbitt turns to me with a nice smile and asks, "So, Iris, how are you doing?"

I blurt out, "Besides seeing the Deets . . . I mean . . . sorry, but anyway . . . it's been the best afternoon of my life!"

Dr. Nesbitt salutes me with his hat. "Do you learn everything this fast?"

"Driving maybe, but not cooking." I smile. "Thank you for teaching me."

We make a deal to practice before supper every evening

until I can go by myself. Dr. Nesbitt gets out, stretches, and kicks the tires.

I stay in the driver's seat for a moment. In my mind I see a ribbon of road rolling away from me, like when I was little staring backward out the car window. A feeling leaps in me, a surge toward something—I don't know what. Driving is like nothing else on earth. I'm not terrible at it. In fact, I love it. I can't believe it, but I do.

But, by far, the very best part of the whole day was just now, when Dr. Nesbitt turned and *asked* me how I was doing rather than telling me.

CHAPTER 10

Mrs. Nesbitt and I cruise through Wellsford with Henry and Marie, the backseat full of supplies: chicken scratch from the feed store; Borax, coffee, evaporated milk, cornmeal, ink, and Wrigley's Gum from Fly's Dry Goods; my silent purchase; and a tank of propane for the range. We have an hour before we pick up Dr. Nesbitt at his office.

Mrs. Nesbitt looks regal in her earrings and embroidered coat. She waves at two little farm boys on the curb. "We need some climbing roses like those," she says over the engine noise, motioning with crumpled fingers toward a brilliant red trellis the color of her jacket. The

owner of the roses swings her watering can at us. Marie
yaps hello.

Dr. Nesbitt knows everybody here—inside and out. But
I wonder what people think of the three of us "ladies" out
on the town without him. I steer past the Presbyterian
Church and cemetery and away from the busy Saturday
morning streets.

I am truly not nervous driving. In fact, it beats riding
any day. I keep the church steeple in sight as we slide past
farmhouses under a lace coverlet of cottonwood shadows.
Out of the corner of my eye even the purple hollyhocks—
privy flowers—bunched around a lonesome outhouse
look royal. We pass a spiny brown ridge that reminds
me of Marie's back when she first arrived, scrubby and
starved. The wind explores the morning, fills my sleeves,
twirls up my skirt, ruffles the robins, then switches des-
tinations, and so do we.

As we crest a hill I feel the earth release us, then hug
us tight going down. Emerald corn fields rustle under
the scalloped telephone wires. I hear rivers of clover hum
the same soft pink note. Everything is moving, talking,
touching above and rooted below. I slow to let a garden
snake show off his swivel dance across the dusty road. Mrs.
Nesbitt pats my arm.

Something brand-new hums in me too. I think it is *joy*.

"Thank you. Thank you . . . I love you," I tell the
mailbox. "Finally, a real, private letter from Leroy!" I

squeeze the envelope. It's fat, at least two pages. My name looks gorgeous written with his pen. I scout around for a private place to read, and decide on Morris's bench.

June 25, 1926
Dear Iris,

Be glad you're not in dull, boring Atchison. My big excitement is watching the goldfish my little sister got for her birthday. She named it Wanda Juanita—because it sounds "watery."

The two older ones mostly act stupid, drooling over Motion Picture Magazine and dreaming up questions to ask me about you? ? ? ?

But guess what? Last week my boss assigned me the railroad repair crew ice route—100 guys living in rail cars. We delivered 5,000 pounds to the cooler in their cook car and got to stay overnight. What a crew! They eat right and know how to make fun out of nothing—talking about girls, playing poker, swapping stories.

News travels down the rails like telephone lines. It's mostly bad—strike threats, cars stalled on the tracks, even a poor old guy struck by lightning.

Besides the ice, I got another job loading dry cement sacks at the docks. I hate it. With me, it's a life of lifting dead weight, whether it's frozen hard or dry as dust. Guess I should have stuck with the piano. Ha!

How'd they talk you into taking over the chicken house? Oh, I know—Mrs. Nesbitt kept pecking at you and you couldn't say no! Please don't tell me you volunteered. Here's your chicken quiz:

Will every egg be a chick if you don't eat it first?

Where are a chicken's teeth?

Which came first: the egg or the dinosaur?

I can see you cruising around cows in Dr. Nesbitt's car.

And you're right—loving to drive is one good thing you inherited from your dad. So finally you found something. Congratulations.

Carl told me he talked to him last week. I really really hope you already know what I'm about to say—your dad told Carl that he and Celeste decided to get married in October and live in Kansas City. Please, please tell me your father already told you. Will they expect you to just pick up and move there in September?

I'll be delivering ice to the crews up by Wellsford real soon. Don't be surprised if I knock on your front door. Maybe you can take me for a ride, if it's okay with Dr. Nesbitt. He sounds real nice.

Until then,
I remain very truly yours,
Leroy Patterson—ice and cement wrestler

P.S. I haven't talked about you to the crew, but I want to.
So there.

I sit on the bench, the letter shaking in both hands. "Well, no, Leroy," I bark at the paper, "of course I did not know already. Why would that . . . *suede salesman* bother to tell me anything?"

I stomp across the driveway and into the chicken house, avoiding Dot, who is stationed at the clothesline. The sharp manure smell shoots up my nose and tears roll down my cheeks. The chickens get blurry. So does my mind. I wipe my face, try to hold my breath, and fumble six eggs into my basket. I shoo a crazy hen pecking her own eggs. "Stop that!" I yell. I feel like ringing her scrawny neck! The coop gets blurry again. *My father.* He does this to me every time. Every single time.

I exit the chicken house.

Dot watches me stuff the letter in my apron pocket.

She glances at Mrs. Nesbitt's bedroom window, glowers at me, and half barks, half whispers, "You just *work* for Dr. Nesbitt. You ain't his daughter. Why'd he teach you to drive? He feels sorry for you." Dot turns her chubby rear to me, stretches on tiptoe to pin the corner of a bath towel to the line. "Why didn't your own daddy teach you? Oh . . ." she turns, puts a finger to her chin, and says in a singsong voice, "that's right . . . he sent you away, didn't he? Well, *my* daddy likes me around all the time. He even had me quit school after Mama passed. Your daddy don't want you, he acts like you're an orphan."

My fingers tighten around the handle of the egg basket. My mouth tastes of chicken grit. Dot's eyes flicker over me. If I didn't know better, I'd swear she had just read Leroy's letter.

She jabs a clothespin at me, lowers her voice. "Plus, where have you got to *go* in that car, anyhow? You ain't got friends or family. Oh, I know, it's so's you can haul Mrs. Snob"— Dot nods toward the window—"to the asylum for nasty old crippled witches who are gonna be dead pretty soon their own selves. Miz Nesbitt already talks to the dead. I've seen her pacin' the porch, chattering to her kilt boy like he was answering back." Dot looks at me, mean and confidential. "*My* daddy says they's queer." She scratches her belly. "He'd never leave me off with them like happened to you!"

Dot puts her hands around her throat and bugs her eyes. "And I heard your mama's been dead so long"—she lolls her head like someone hanging from a noose—"if you talked to her, she'd never answer. She's just a bag of double moldy bones."

I open my mouth then snap it shut.

"You're *nothin'* to no one, Iris Baldwin."

I take a deep breath, bite my lip.

Dot turns back to her laundry. I watch the crimson target of her fuzzy hair bob against the row of sheets and towels. My fingers search the basket, curl around an egg.

In a flash it explodes off the back of Dot's head.

She jerks forward. Plants her feet. Growls. Squeezes her fists. It's deathly quiet except for the drum of my heart. I brace against the fence. She's going to kill me. But, odd as can be, she doesn't turn around. She just swipes her hands on her sack dress and finishes hanging the towel.

A chicken struts herky-jerky between us. It cocks its head and ruffles its tail at the bits of shell and egg innards dangling from Dot's red frizz like tinsel in the sun.

My chest heaves. I turn and burst into the house. The shotgun propped by the door slides down and clatters on the floor. Mrs. Nesbitt will be out of her bedroom any minute. I watch Dot from the window. She drops her apron full of clothespins in the dirt, spits, and ambles off toward home, leaving a pile of wet sheets in the basket.

I scurry past Mrs. Nesbitt's bedroom door and hide out in my room. I grab Rosie and hug her until I stop shaking. On the dresser is the letter I started to my father and Celeste yesterday. I had tried to write them something newsy that would help Celeste get to know me a little bit, like Mrs. Nesbitt hinted maybe I should do. Well, that'll be a trick, because until today I had never met the Iris who threw that egg.

July 2, 1926
Dear Father and Celeste,

I told the Nesbitts of your engagement. They send congratulations.

How is the store progressing? Someday I will see the results of all your hard window-dressing work. I am now in charge of the chicken house—a spot that definitely needed attention. It's not exactly a high-style shoe store, but the birds are finally getting used to me and their day-to-day routine.

In answer to your question, Dr. Nesbitt drives a Ford Model T Tudor Sedan. It's black. He taught me to drive, which I took right to. I think I inherited a love of driving from you. Who'd have thought we had that in common? How do you like your Cadillac?

Do you talk with Carl? I miss him and the store. . . .

The letter makes me sick. In every sentence I am pushing the pen uphill. I rip it up. Phony. *Phony.* It sounds like Celeste helped me write it. Me trying to add her into our "family" has made what there was of it disappear.

I scrape my pen across a fresh sheet of paper. It's not a push this time. That egg-throw feeling still pulses through my arm.

July 2, 1926
Dear Father,

I am aware of your engagement news. Dr. Nesbitt drives a Model T.
I didn't recieve a letter from you regarding your wedding date in October and your decision to stay in Kansas City. Did you mean to write or call me but just forgot?

Iris

I misspell the words on purpose. It'll drive him crazy. My handwriting looks wobbly, but I fold the letter into an envelope and walk it straight down the driveway to the mailbox. I leave pennies for postage. I hope it hits him as hard as a dozen eggs, but I know it won't. It's like throwing rocks at God.

I sit on the side of the ditch, hidden by corn and cattails. I hold my stomach, which feels like a coiled snake squeezing my organs to death. Grasshoppers leap on me, ticking and buzzing. The mailbox flag rattles when a truck rumbles by. When I was little I believed that grasshoppers spit real tobacco juice. How dumb was that? As dumb as believing I ever had a real home in Atchison to go back to. As stupid as wasting an egg on Dot. When I tell the Nesbitts what I did they'll fire me. What else can they do? The Deets were here first, they live here. Mrs. Nesbitt still feels so guilty about Pansy leaving, she's got to take Dot's side.

I hear Marie trot down the driveway. She sniffs me out, then sits—not a comfortable, resting type of sit, but alert and protective. Her tail stub thumps the dirt.

I hug her. "I guess you know as well as anybody how this feels," I say, "being a hobo just sitting in a ditch."

CHAPTER 11

"I beaned Dot," I say *too quickly and too loudly the* minute we sit down to supper.

Dr. and Mrs. Nesbitt look at me like I've just lit a cigar.

I stare at my lap, wave a fly off my sweet potatoes. "W-w-with an egg." All eyes, even Marie's, are pairs of question marks. "I've never hit anybody before . . . ever. I just . . ." I grip my napkin.

Mrs. Nesbitt gives me a long look I can't read the meaning of. Dr. Nesbitt pushes away from the table, walks to the screen door, and stares off into the cornfields. He rises slightly on his toes, makes a fist. He looks mad. Marie trots over beside Mrs. Nesbitt, who covers her mouth with her napkin.

"Back here? Did it happen in the yard?" Dr. Nesbitt asks abruptly, stepping onto the back porch.

"Yes, sir."

He motions for me to come out. "Where was Dot?"

I point to the clothesline pole. "I brought in the laundry," I say feebly. "She left without reporting her count."

"And where were you?" he asks. I point again. He shields his eyes from the setting sun and paces the distance between the chicken fence and the clothesline. Then he marches past me back into the house.

We sit at the table. Mrs. Nesbitt waves her fan against the drippy heat. We've still not eaten a bite. Marie acts as confused as I am. She pokes at her dish of scraps and looks up, as if asking, *Is it okay to eat now?*

Dr. Nesbitt flicks his mother a look, then stabs a pickled okra.

I put down my fork.

Dr. and Mrs. Nesbitt eat quietly. Nobody comments on the sweet potatoes that I've made for the first time. No one asks about dessert. No one asks why I did it.

"Dot was right, Avery," Mrs. Nesbitt says after a long, awful silence.

My face burns. My hands tingle. I stand, ready to flee the room. *"Ma'am?"* My voice shakes. "How could you say that?

"I *am* crippled and I do, or at least I did, talk to Morris and pace the porch. When Morris addresses me," she says matter-of-factly, "it's impolite, even for a snob, not to answer. I just so happened to have finished conversing with 'the dead' this morning in time to hear every word of Dot's assessment of us through my bedroom window."

I catch my breath. Dr. Nesbitt mops his forehead with his handkerchief. He looks up at me, his face dead serious. "Did Miss Deets insult you in every way a fellow human being possibly could?"

"Yes."

"Did she attack things precious to you?"

Mrs. Nesbitt chimes in. "Of course she did, Avery."

"So essentially, Iris, she hit you first."

I look down at the perfect part in Dr. Nesbitt's hair.

"It seems Miss Deets felt all too qualified to assess *you*," he says. "What do you think of *her*?"

I shuffle my feet. "She's half rat."

Dr. Nesbitt nods and stands to face me. "An egg's trajectory is wobbly at best. Hitting your target at twenty-five paces requires skill." He holds me in his strong gaze, tips his water glass. "Well done."

Trouble.

I shoot straight up in bed, my head filled with Dot and the egg and how she acted so strange, as though she was used to getting hit.

I grab my pillow, thinking . . .

Did Dot lure me right into a trap, make me do something to get fired? Or did she tell Cecil about it, get him all stirred up, put me on his bad side—as if there were a *good* one. Someday, somehow, he'll pay me back. Maybe that's why she stopped, didn't wipe her hair . . . so she could say, "See what Iris did? She started it."

I shiver, imagining how shifty they all are, how Cecil treated his own wife. I know they would turn on anybody—the Nesbitts, me, even each other.

An egg and a good aim won't be enough for Cecil Deets.

July 12, 1926
Dear Iris,

Would you believe our store is less than a month away from the grand opening on August 10th? Could you possibly come for it? I imagine you've made yourself indispensable to the Nesbitts. Could they spare you a few days?

How is the elderly woman in your care? I so admire you for going about your day-to-day without the modern conveniences. Kansas City has such a climate of refinement and urban sophistication. Wouldn't you leap at the opportunity to live here?

Our wedding plans, besides deciding on the date, have taken a backseat to getting Baldwin's Bootery (yes, we did decide) running. Our marriage will be October 10th—your 16th birthday! What a grand way to celebrate both occasions.

Let us know if you need anything at all, dear. Sounds like you made a good choice with Wellsford, but do please give Kansas City a fighting chance.

Love,
Celeste

P. S. Our store windows have garnered lots of attention. You know your father—he needs to be first, fastest, and farthest in whatever he does. Why, sometimes even I have trouble keeping up!

Wellsford. A *choice*? She thinks *I* picked Wellsford? What a "refined" way my father has of twisting the truth.

Well, no, Celeste, I do not want to come to the grand opening. Nor do I want to live with you two in the Paris of the Plains. And, most unfortunately, I accidentally left my suede footwear on the train, which makes a sophisticated leap into Kansas City absolutely impossible!

CHAPTER 12

"Don't you dare laugh, Marie."

She tracks my rolling pin back and forth and sniffs the doughy bits I drop for her. "This isn't *squirrel stew*. I'm practicing. It's going to be a delicate pie crust. I'd like to see you try and make one."

I'm working to keep my mind off Dot, who will be here any minute to start the laundry. The Nesbitts decided to take "the high road" and not fire her, but I think it's because nobody wanted to do it.

I hear the Rawleigh man's wagon in the driveway. Marie trots to the kitchen door, but her friendly *yap-yap* turns to a growl.

"Shhh . . . Mrs. Nesbitt's asleep. Don't scare him off. He's nice. I've got a list. . . ."

But Marie is about to tear through the screen.

It's Cecil, alone, in his wagon.

The egg. My mouth turns to cotton.

Cecil's horse pees on our yard. Cecil squints at the empty shed, then spots me through the kitchen door. "The Doc here?" he yells, his voice high and edgy.

Why's he asking? He can see *the Doc's* car is gone. I open the door enough for Marie to slip out. "No."

He cranes his neck toward me, scowls. "Didn't hear ya."

I step partway onto the porch. "I said, *no.*" I silently order Marie to chew Cecil to stew meat if he makes the tiniest move off his seat.

He smirks at her clown-dog nose smudged with flour. He teases one foot off the wagon, which sends her into spasms of snarling. But he stays put on the bench. His face looks ragged. He winces, shifts his weight like the plank seat has sprouted splinters, and adjusts the front of his overalls. *Get out of here.*

Cecil takes an eternity to dig a tobacco pouch from inside the bib of his overalls and sticks a wad in his cheek. He picks leaf flecks off his bottom lip. I wonder what stories about me lurk under that dirty straw hat. "Dot's not comin' today," he remarks, scanning the yard like he owns the place. "She's feeling . . . poorly."

I don't ask what's the matter with Dot. "Dr. Nesbitt's at his office. You can take her there."

He shrugs, then slaps the reins on his palm, his eyes

shifting between the clothesline, the chicken house, and me. *Leave!*

He glances at Mrs. Nesbitt's shaded window and leans toward me, a glint in his eye. He whispers, "I hear you're a feisty one. . . ."

I wish I had the rolling pin in my fist. I wish the sheriff was in the kitchen with his rifle loaded. But before Cecil can utter another word, an angel, in the form of the Rawleigh man in his buggy, stops at the bottom of our driveway.

Cecil grimaces, throws his hands up, and without another word forces his horse to make a tight turn around. His wagon stops halfway down the driveway. The Rawleigh man waits while Cecil folds a horse blanket and gingerly tucks it under himself on the seat. The medicine salesman tips his hat—"Mr. Deets"—but he shakes his head in a sorry kind of way after Cecil passes onto the road toward town.

The Rawleigh gentleman stands down from his buggy and scratches Marie's ears. I read our list. "We need Camphor Balm and Bee Secret." He sorts through his sample cases. "What's that Anti-Pain Oil for?" I ask, spotting a row of dark bottles.

"The Internal or the External?" the Rawleigh man asks.

"External."

"It's for rheumatism."

"I'll take a bottle for Mrs. Nesbitt's hands." I run inside and get cash from my pocketbook. It'll be a present.

He explains his assortment of penetrating rubs made with oils from Sicily, perfumes from Mexico, Japanese camphor, and eucalyptus. "W. T. Rawleigh searches everywhere for his scientific ingredients. A far cry from the usual *folk* remedies." He rolls his eyes. "No doubt Mrs. Nesbitt has tried dozens of those, too."

"I don't know, sir."

"In my business I've heard every remedy known to man. Course, Doc Nesbitt probably has too. . . ." He looks up. "Let's see, for rheumatism . . . put a teaspoonful of salt in your shoe. Wear a bull snake tied around your waist or—*my favorite*—if afflicted with rheumatism, sleep with a dog wrapped around your feet, and the rheumatism will drain into the dog." He tips his head apologetically at Marie. "I guess that means you, dear."

I smile. "We'll try the massage instead."

"You'd better do that in red flannel pajamas with an acorn in your pocket." He climbs in his buggy, circles the driveway, and stops. "Or there's always tying a woolen string just below the knee, or rubbing a cow's gall bladder on the afflicted joints . . ."

I make a face. "Maybe next time. Thank you," I yell as he wheels past the mailbox.

"Seems Cecil's rear end is what's feeling poorly today," I whisper to Marie as we go inside with our purchases. "What's the folk remedy for *that*, I'd like to know?"

I sort our unusually large and nasty pile of laundry. Except for the lipstick on Mrs. Nesbitt's hankies, it looks like a load from a railroad repair crew—greasy rags, a frayed cook's apron soaked with blackberry juice, even a hand towel caked with Marie's muddy paw prints.

"Mrs. Nesbitt?" I say as she and Henry step out by the washing machine. "It looks like we used these napkins for tea bags. And what did Marie get into?" I pinch the corner of an especially smelly scrap of blanket from Marie's bed.

"Sorry, dear." She looks down. "We're guilty." Mrs. Nesbitt glances at Marie. "Both of us. I . . . *we* so looked forward to Dot having to do all this awful wash. Payback for the mess *she* made. A bit pathetic, perhaps . . . but"—her eyes light up—"the girl asked for it." She points with Henry. "Oh, and look in the bottom, you'll find the dishcloths we glued together with egg yolk. Not to worry. They're all just rags you can throw out."

"Very clever," I say the way Dr. Nesbitt would. I raise the Borax to her. "Well done."

Since I've dusted her glasses a hundred times without breaking them, Mrs. Nesbitt says she trusts me to massage her fragile fingers with the oil. We sit, turned toward each other, on a cushion in the old spring wagon seat by the birdbath—the place Mrs. Nesbitt likes to ask me hard questions in a soft way. I keep an eye on the driveway, for fear Cecil will come rolling up.

Her hands across a pillow on my lap look like wilted hibiscus blooms.

The Anti-Pain Oil brings the smells of the whole wide world into the palm of my hand. Marie sniffs it, sneezes. I tell Mrs. Nesbitt about the exotic ingredients. "Ah, the sweet life you might have had with a French or a Japanese hobo," she says to Marie, who sneezes again. "By the way, do you two know what 'hobo' really means?"

"No, ma'am."

"It means 'homeward bound.'" She sits back, closes her eyes. I fumble her fingers apart and begin to work the oil. Like tumblers inside a frozen lock, her joints loosen a little. "And," she says, "that's exactly how we felt—like hobos, when Avery and I came to live here after Morris died. We came home *for* Morris, since he couldn't." She grips my hand. "He was lost at sea . . . a German U-boat."

My thoughts travel to Morris, drifting and bumping forever across the floor of the Atlantic in his uniform, then to Mama, all dressed up in her earthly coffin home in Kansas. I shake the images away. "I'm so very sorry, Mrs. Nesbitt." We gaze at the sturdy tugboat of a farmhouse Morris built, anchored in this sunny green ocean of grass and corn.

She smiles sadly. "Would you like to know what I say to him?"

"Morris?"

"Yes, when I pace the porch and talk to him. May I tell you what I say?"

"Yes, ma'am, please."

"I apologize for being so angry at the world for his dying, for being miserable and morbid for so long. I turned my angel into a ghost." She wipes her eyes. "So Avery, bless his heart, who has had his own grief to bear, finally wrote a *prescription* for me. A folk remedy, so to speak. And here you are! He knew I needed a person, not a pill."

Mrs. Nesbitt places both her hands on mine. We sit silent for a long while.

The words tumble from my mouth before I can stop them. "*I* have a person—sort of a friend—who might come visit me here, if it's all right."

"From home?"

"Yes, ma'am." My face is hot. So are the soles of my feet and everyplace in between.

"So tell me about her, Iris."

"Her name is . . . Leroy."

Mrs. Nesbitt turns with her mouth open.

"P-P-Patterson. Leroy Patterson," I sputter. I swear I have never said his whole name out loud before.

"So *she's* of the male persuasion." Mrs. Nesbitt smiles.

"He's got three sisters. He knows a lot about girls. . . ."

"Interesting."

"I don't mean he's *known* a lot of girls, I mean he's . . ." I want to swallow every word, curl up, and die.

"How old is Leroy Patterson?"

"Almost eighteen. He's good at lifting, or he could pull something heavy for you, like cement, or maybe help with chores, or . . ." Leroy sounds like a donkey, and I sound worse than Celeste would trying to sell a pair of used work boots.

"Please invite him, Iris."

"Yes, ma'am. Maybe I'll do that. Thank you."

"I'd like to go to Atchison with you sometime," Miss Nesbitt says softly. "See your home."

I inhale sharply, shift on the bench. "My father is going to sell it."

The Anti-Pain Oil radiates across our hands.

"I'm trying not to think about it," I say. But longing washes over me. I want to go there this minute and dust it. There's so much I can't say right now. Too many empty places to fill. I want to ask Mrs. Nesbitt what she'll do in September when I'm gone, but I don't. I can't think about that either. Clouds hover over the house.

Her tone is halting, careful. "Tell me about your mother, Iris?"

I slip my hands back. "I . . . she . . ."

Mrs. Nesbitt seems suddenly interested in a jumble of elm branches dipping in the wind. She passes me her hankie.

"She was always so sick. I wasn't allowed to touch her."

"Did your father ever tell stories about her, or . . . ?"

"Never."

Mrs. Nesbitt studies me. Her eyes are sea gray. I imagine Morris in them.

Mrs. Nesbitt says, "You know, Iris—Morris, your mama, Marie, you, me, why even Pansy Deets, we're all hobos. Homeward bound."

Dr. Nesbitt squats by a wagon rut in the grass and frowns. "Was Cecil by here today?"

I shudder. "Yes, sir. And the narrow tracks are the Rawleigh man's buggy."

"Did Dot come?"

"No."

Dr. Nesbitt looks up at me, his face troubled, his white broadcloth shirt still neat as a pin after a long day at work. "Did Cecil act strange?"

"Of course he acted strange. He's Cecil," Mrs. Nesbitt says. "Why?"

"He came to my office."

"With Dot?" I ask. "She's sick."

"No." Dr. Nesbitt shakes his head. "Cecil didn't say anything about Dot. He has a horrible case of hemorrhoids."

"Sir?"

"This is a bit medical, Iris, but I know you can manage it. Hemorrhoids are a painful inflammation of the buttocks." I swear I see a trace of mischief in Dr. Nesbitt's expression. "The vessels of the rump."

I work furiously to fight off the picture forming in my mind.

Mrs. Nesbitt screws up her face. "Is the inflammation everywhere? . . . I hope."

"Well no, Mother, it's . . ." He squeezes his fist.

Mrs. Nesbitt waves her hand. "Never mind. At least, for once, we're not hearing your grisly diagnosis at the *dinner table*."

"So *that's* why Cecil showed up this morning." I shiver. "Why, he acted like a rooster trying to lay an egg. I thought he was after revenge for my hitting Dot."

I can't tell them how he leers at me, how I think he might touch me if he thought he could get away with it.

Mrs. Nesbitt's eyes sparkle. "Did you treat the affected rump, Avery?"

"Yes. Consider Cecil all tied up, at least for now. But"—his expression darkens—"Cecil's spleen is enlarged too. Most likely he's drinking again."

Mrs. Nesbitt sighs. "His drinking is even worse since Pansy left, isn't it, Avery?"

Dr. Nesbitt shrugs. "Mother, Cecil Deets's moonshine habit is not your fault."

Mrs. Nesbitt looks skyward, bounces her fist off her lap. "Why didn't Dot go with her mother?"

"We'll never know. That's not your fault either."

I can't help imagining Dot day in, day out, at home with Cecil—listening to him rant against Pansy, sneaking past his drunken gaze, bracing against his grip, growing as mean and sly as he is.

One thing I do know: Cecil Deets makes my father seem like a sweet dream.

CHAPTER 13

Ghosts rattle the roof—Wake up!

I sit up, still half in my dream.

Your house! Read the sign.

I untwist my nightgown, open the sheers, and gaze out the window. Hail hammers the shingles. Lightning turns the ice stones to a field of opals. But my dream-eyes focus on something else: my front yard back in Atchison with a FOR SALE sign on it.

I drop my head. Dread creeps up from the cellar inside me, the place where every miserable, morbid thing lives. It's crowded down there and locked. But Mrs. Nesbitt's questions about Mama and my house forced the FOR SALE sign to escape through the dream door.

Daddy's selling our past. At least my nightmare of living with Celeste in Atchison won't happen.

I hug my knees, wanting the bedroom to fold in around me, to wall off the future.

My fingers trace the imaginary ribs of my old chenille bedspread. I smell the faint bacon grease and coffee scent of our kitchen.

Staccato pops of hail on the window glass force me back to Wellsford. Marie hops in my lap. "Maybe he'll sell me with the house," I tell her. "Why not?" She curls up while I shudder and sob. It's storming inside, too. "Do you miss your hobo?" I scratch her ears. "He was loyal. At least you two worked *together*." I light my lamp, a glimmer of mad beginning to mingle with morbid, and write.

July 30, 1926
Dear Leroy,

Please answer immediately. Is there a "For Sale" sign in my front yard? I've got to know. I dreamed it was true, so the idea is stuck in my brain like a sliver. Daddy is not going to rent our house—he's selling it, isn't he?

You always tell me the things I need to

know, the truth. So be warned, I'm counting on you.

Here's a quiz—if it's true about Atchison. (Which I'm sure it is.)

Question: If you take mad, and multiply it by ignored plus tricked, what do you have?

Answer: Guess who?

Question: What's the worst kind of homesick?

Answer: Homesick for something you wanted that never was.

Signed:

Iris Baldwin, ~~the shadow in her father's~~ palace of grand plans

P.S. The Nesbitts are happy for you to visit. The sooner the better. They promise to have lots of dead weight for you to lift. Ha!

P.P.S. I'll make you a pie. Really! Blackberry or rhubarb. You pick.

P.P.P.S. Write me back with the answer right now.

P.P.P.P.S. How are you?

I've counted on Leroy for the truth ever since the sixth grade, when he set me straight about virgins.

"So, okay, what exactly is a virgin?" I had asked him. "Isn't it a lady who hasn't had a baby—like the Virgin Mary?"

"Oh God, Iris." Leroy searched my face, to see if I was kidding, I guess. "Did you look it up?"

"The Bible doesn't have a glossary!"

"In the *dictionary*."

"Yes, but the definitions go in word circles. You have *sisters*, Leroy. You're thirteen. You know the answer. So tell me!"

He did. He just explained sexual intercourse and what a virgin isn't. It was the bravest thing.

"So no wonder Daddy blew like he'd eaten a tablespoon of pepper when I asked if his girlfriend was a virgin," I had said. Leroy smiled. "Daddy dropped her on a dime—thought I'd heard rumors about her rep-u-ta-tion! Couldn't stand the risk of a blemish on *his*."

"Well, at least you got his attention for once," Leroy had commented.

I scratch Marie's back, thinking maybe I should ask Daddy about Celeste's virgin status. I could get rid of her, too.

Dot's back.

After weeks of feeling ill, she has her sack dress hiked up in the back and pulled tighter across her belly than Cecil's overalls. She is definitely not over her *poorly*-ness. Already this morning she's gotten sick to her stomach three times. From the chicken house I've seen Marie follow her between the clothesline and the grassy patch behind the shed. I've heard Dot retch, watched her wobble back to the laundry, her back soaked with sweat.

I abandon my broom and exit the coop. The door bangs shut. Dot turns, glances at my hand as if checking for an egg, and yanks down her dress. She looks pale. Her hair looks dirty and there are dark circles under her eyes. When she reaches to shove a clothespin on the line, I see marks on her arms.

Bruises.

My stomach twists.

Dot turns to face me, plants her fists on her hips, stretches her back, and sticks her stomach out. Then she lifts the hair off her neck with one hand, fans it with the other.

More bruises.

Without a word, she looks me right in the eye, rubs the fingertips of both hands back and forth across her belly, then glances toward the shed.

A notion—a knowing—slips into my mind.

Dot is pregnant.

Marie barks at crows filling the telephone line.

Dot turns away, bends over, and presses the heels of her hands on her eyes. Her shoulders raise and lower.

Is she *crying*? "Dot?" My voice sounds unexpectedly soft, like Mrs. Nesbitt's.

"Shut up!"

Dot spits, wipes her mouth, and after a moment snipes, "Oh, and by the way, *you're* gonna be gone in a week." She resumes pinning clothes as if giving me a generous moment of privacy to absorb *my own* nasty news.

"I saw the letter." Her tone shifts to *poor, poor Iris*. "Your replacement's name is Gladys Dilgert. It's right on the envelope. They've kept it a secret from you, but it's in plain sight on the kitchen table." She shoos me off. "Go see for yourself."

I glue my lips. I will not ask one question.

"I know you're wonderin' if I opened the letter and read it." Dot glances at the telephone line. "Didn't need to. I know what's in it."

I turn to Mrs. Nesbitt's bedroom window, praying it's open, that she and Henry will pop through and whack Dot in her lying vocal cords.

"So . . ." Dot flaps a pudgy hand. "Toodle-loo, Miss Iris Baldwin." She hums a mocking little melody.

I walk, slow as molasses, back into the house.

There's no mail on the kitchen table, only a cold tea bag and Mrs. Nesbitt's unfinished crossword. I know she has already taken the mail to Dr. Nesbitt's bedroom desk, the one room in this house, besides the abandoned fruit cellar, I have never entered.

I'm worse than Dot wearing two faces, because during Mrs. Nesbitt's afternoon nap I do what I swear I wouldn't.

I sneak straight to Dr. Nesbitt's desk to read mail that's not mine.

It's tidy and nice. A gentleman's room, I guess, with a polished mahogany wardrobe and a shaving set on the dresser. I avoid the mail stack for a moment, concentrate on his desk photographs. One man looks interesting—a handsome artist at his easel. The other picture is all doctors—graduates of Johns Hopkins Medical School. Dr. Nesbitt smiles amidst a sea of seriousness. There's also a large picture of Morris, in a Navy uniform, and an older gentleman, who looks like Dr. Nesbitt and Morris combined. A silver rack holds ivory envelopes with smooth script. They must be from his lady friend in New York. I wonder why there is no picture of her, but I can't ask. Dr. Nesbitt cleans his own room for a reason: to keep his private business private.

The envelope is lost in plain sight on the blotter. It's got the return address of Gladys Dilgert, just like Dot said. I do not touch it.

Beside it, tucked into the flap of a leather-bound notepad, I see a small newspaper copy of Dr. Nesbitt's latest want ad, a solicitation for hired help to begin in September. The name Dilgert is written on the pad along with a number. He made the arrangements on the telephone and Dot must have overheard it, probably eavesdropping on the party line.

I'm burning up. I hate Dot. She's fat and cruel . . . and right.

What's the folk remedy for this feeling, I wonder? Goose grease on the heart? Swallowing a falling star?

The old cellar ghosts rattle. "Feeling like a piece of furniture," "Replaceable," and "Homeless" line up. But instead they seep out of my eyes, which are still swollen later when Mrs. Nesbitt calls from the yard.

It's time for our hand massage.

We sit on the bench. The lawn is littered with hail-shredded leaves. Our marigold patch is battered and muddy. The house winks at us—a flutter of lace waving from my bedroom, next to the dark parlor window shut tight.

I'm sure Mrs. Nesbitt can tell I've been crying. She must feel the warmth drained from our massage today. She sits with her pretty, old, crinkly face and penetrating eyes, ready to chat. But I'm too sunk inside to talk. Being sold out by my father is rotten enough, but now the Nesbitts . . .

I'm stupid for thinking they wouldn't hire somebody else. Of course they would. Mrs. Nesbitt just needs *someone,* not me—Gladys or anyone could become the new goddess of the chicken house this fall. I'm doomed to Kansas City with Mrs. Charles Baldwin and her charming new husband. I need to quickly crawl in my trunk, ship myself somewhere far down the tracks.

Still, I want to ask Mrs. Nesbitt: *Why didn't you tell me, warn me about Miss Dilgert?* Gladys's ghost, with its nimble fingers and projecting personality, has already moved between us on the bench. I had planned to tell Mrs. Nesbitt about my For Sale—sign nightmare, but I don't. I just stare at my bedroom window. I can already *see* Gladys in there, wearing my Pompeian Body Powder.

Mrs. Nesbitt squeezes my hand. Without realizing it, I've stopped rubbing. "Are you all right, dear?"

"No."

Mrs. Nesbitt takes a deep breath and looks at me in the kindest way. I feel pressure from her thumbs in the palms of my hands. But she doesn't ask me what's wrong. Instead she gives me a long silent moment to fill with an explanation if I choose.

I don't. I can't talk about anything—not Dot or Gladys. Inside and out, life is just not holding together like it's supposed to.

Mrs. Nesbitt gazes at the house, then off toward the clothesline. "Would you guess I used to play the piano?" she says, turning her hands. "So did Morris. He had a gift."

I imagine Morris's piano music pouring out that parlor window. I want to ask if Gladys Dilgert plays piano, but I don't. "Is Morris the reason we never dust the piano or the parlor, you know . . . like we do your bedroom things?"

"Yes."

Now I know why the front room holds its dusty breath, why the cover on the piano keys stays down. It's still Morris's room. She's preserving his fingerprints.

We move to the kitchen. Mrs. Nesbitt wants help with her puzzle. She slides me a pencil and squints at the crossword. "For some reason I've had such difficulty with this today, Iris. Explosive. Second letter is 'y.'"

"Dynamite," I say. I fill in "mule" and "superstition."

"How was your encounter with Dot this morning?" she asks.

"Her mouth is lethal." I grind the words. "And she's still sick . . ."

"Yes . . . ?" Mrs. Nesbitt folds her hands on the table.

I sense another invitation to say what's on my mind. I glue my eyes to the crossword and like a magical omen, there it is. "Twenty-four down—expecting," I whisper.

"Anticipating."

I count out the squares. "No. It's only nine letters." My stomach is a knot. "Mrs. Nesbitt? Uh . . . the answer is '*with child*'—the letters all run together."

"Ah . . . yes. Good!"

"No," I say slowly, "not so good."

She searches my face. "What is it, Iris?"

I picture Dot today and how she'll look in the coming months. "I mean, have you noticed that Dot's gotten bigger around the middle even though she's been so sick?"

"Dot?"

"Yes, ma'am. Dot." Tears fill my eyes. The words burst out. "I think she's *with child*."

Mrs. Nesbitt twists her hankie while I tell her about the bruises on Dot's arms and neck and the unforgettable way she touched her stomach. "I think she was telling me, without saying it. The way Pansy showed you her bruises."

Mrs. Nesbitt looks at the ceiling. "Couldn't it just be a buildup of bad humors?"

"In a way, yes."

"But . . . who?" Mrs. Nesbitt sounds frantic and resigned. "The Deets keep so to themselves. Dot doesn't know anybody much. Since Pansy left it seems her only connection to the outside world is listening on the party line and our laundry. When my glasses are clean I don't miss much, but this . . . is all my fault!"

We fall silent a moment. "Poorly isn't all she's going to feel when Cecil finds out," she says. "He's already drinking himself to death, crazier every day . . . he'll . . . Oh, God." She shakes her head.

We pile our hands on the faded oil cloth and bow our heads, the crossword puzzle forgotten.

CHAPTER 14

It's Saturday morning and Dr. Nesbitt has mowed the lawn, trimmed the hedge, and swept the stoop—all before breakfast.

It's steamy hot with no breeze. "If he starts chopping firewood," Mrs. Nesbitt says, fanning herself at the kitchen table, "I'm calling a doctor!"

I smile and weave my mending needle into a frayed milking smock Mrs. Nesbitt plans to give Dot. I don't know how she's going to do it though, since we've been acting like Dot doesn't have that unspeakable baby growing inside her.

Mrs. Nesbitt folds her hands and says matter-of-factly, "He knows."

I stare a hole through her. "Cecil knows about Dot?"

"No, Iris, *Avery* knows." She glances out the window at her son marching toward the house with the freshly oiled shotgun. She whispers fast. "He told me he'd figured it out. That's why he's so wound up, why we all are . . ." She shakes her head.

Dr. Nesbitt steps in, props the gun by the door, his expression grim. "Mother, could you please stay by the phone. I'm expecting a call anytime. I think I'll have a delivery today."

Before I can catch it, "*Dot*?" pops out of my mouth. We sit a moment surrounded by my stunning stupidity. "Of course it's not Dot . . . yet," I blubber. "I'm sorry. She's not . . . I won't . . ."

Cows bawl. Wasps float around their nest in the window casement.

"I know, Iris. Dot seems to be the only girl in the whole world expecting a baby," Mrs. Nesbitt says.

Dr. Nesbitt swipes his hands on his work pants. "Well, Cora started labor prematurely. I think I heard two heartbeats last week. Twins run in Ellis's family. I'd like you to come along to help, Iris."

My stomach drops. I poke the needle in my finger, my face hot and undoubtedly as red as the bright bubble of blood I blot on my napkin. "Yes, sir," I say, trying to imagine how I can do anything useful besides boil water and wring my fingers into knots.

I catch Mrs. Nesbitt watching me. "You give an excellent hand massage. I am sure you will do wonderfully."

Dr. Nesbitt nods and crunches down the driveway for the mail. Moments later he plops a Sears and Roebuck catalog and a letter for me on the table and carries the rest to his room. Celeste's handwriting.

Ugh . . .

I stuff the envelope in my pocket. It can wait.

Mrs. Nesbitt and I get busy too, as though chores can make Dot go away. But I know busyness won't erase Celeste, or Dot's baby, or my impossible awkwardness. And all the busywork in the world can't stop the train to Kansas City in September with me on board.

Just the same, I straighten the linen closet, reline Mrs. Nesbitt's hankie box with fresh paper, gather eggs, and make corn muffins. I even give Marie a bath with Dr. Nesbitt's car-washing water. We clean out the pantry and pack the backseat of the car with canned peaches and apple butter and a cardboard box of old quilt scraps and towels. Dr. Nesbitt adds his flashlight, extra batteries, his black bag, and a box of matches. This could be quite a night.

Long after supper the telephone rings, and we're off.

The steamy heat has collected itself into droplets that wash the windshield as we navigate our way to Cora's.

Standing on the worn wood porch are a yellow cat and Ellis, Cora's lanky husband. Both look like they've been living on an empty stomach. "Cora's water shed," Ellis mumbles, bumping his head on the door frame as we go inside.

While Dr. Nesbitt examines her, I boil water, refold the rags, and avoid the bedroom. Finally he calls me in.

I stop dead away at the door. A boggy, toadstool smell mixes with Cora's moaning and panting. She's dark-haired and ghosty-white with a fistful of damp bedding in each hand.

I step back. Dim curtains draw around my eyes. I grab the door handle and count my breaths.

Cora turns toward me, wild-eyed. She blinks to focus and whispers hoarsely, "Get Ruthie. She's scarit. Thinks I'm dyin'."

Dr. Nesbitt and I turn to Ellis. "Ruthie?"

Cora's husband looks for a moment as though he can't place who that is. He bends down and yells under the bed. "Ruth, come out from there this minute!"

We wait.

"Ruth!" He swipes his long arm. "The doctor's here. I said get out."

Something stirs in me. "Please. I'll take care of her," I hear myself offer. I squat down and lift the dingy bed skirt. In deep shadow I make out a figure curled on her side. Above us, the mattress sags under the writhing weight of her mother and two unborn babies, who also seem scared to face the world.

I have an idea. I go in the front room and unload the quilts. With a pair of scissors from Dr. Nesbitt's bag, I cut a paper doll girl and two tiny baby shapes out of the cardboard box.

Flat on my stomach, I poke my head under the bed. I sweep the flashlight and come face to face with Ruthie. I hold the paper doll up to the light and jiggle her like she's talking. "Hi, Ruthie, would you like a corn muffin?"

Ruthie glues her eyes to the doll. Says nothing.

"Or would you like something to hold?" the doll asks.

Ruthie doesn't move.

I slide a quilt scrap across the dusty plywood.

Ruthie pops her thumb in her mouth. She stares at me with perfectly round pale eyes. We stay there together a long while—with me stretched out right in Dr. Nesbitt's path around the bed. I guess he'll step on me if he needs my help.

Cora's growls turn to shrieks. "I think Mother Nature can hear you now," Dr. Nesbitt says. "Good job. She's ready to lend a hand with these babies."

I stretch my arm and walk the little figure toward Ruthie. "Can I lay down with you?" I say in my dolly voice. She takes the cutout and examines her in the flashlight beam.

I hear Dr. Nesbitt unlatch his black bag and rattle through it. "Damn . . . damn," he whispers. I lift the bed skirt and look out. His yard shoes squeak as he steps over me. The tan leather is scarred and soft. Next thing I know he's yanking out his shoelaces.

I turn back and show Ruthie the two lumpy cardboard baby shapes. "Hi, sister," they say.

She giggles and reaches for them.

"We want to hug you." Ruthie presses the cardboard girl against the babies.

Something's happening. The weight of Cora has moved toward the foot of the bed. Dr. Nesbitt calls Ellis in from the front room. There are no newborn cries, only a new smell of wet, rusted iron—blood, earth, and sweat.

"Would you like to come out now?" I ask Ruthie.

She shakes her head no.

"That's fine," I say. "I'll be right back." I go to the kitchen and spread twin corn muffins with apple butter, put them on a plate. I carry the plate to the bedroom, kneel down, and push it across to Ruthie. She eats the muffins flat on her back, drizzling crumbs like rain. I smile. "I'll bet the mice love you."

In a moment Ruthie collects her dollies and quilt and crawls out. Her curly strawberry hair is matted to her face.

I carry her right out to the back porch. There's no swing, so I feel for the step in the pitch-dark. Tree toads and crickets saw the humid air. I cradle her on my lap. I smell muffin crumbs and dusty little-girl sweat in her hair. The weight of sleep fills her legs, her back, and finally her head. I stroke her downy cheek. I make the rhythm of our breaths match.

The huge oak overhead drops its acorns on the yard. An owl floats his question across the fertile night. *Hoo? Hoo?*

Through the window I hear Dr. Nesbitt instruct Ellis. "These babies need your help." His voice is kind and wise, like a traveler sure of his destination. "Okay, Cora, Ellis is going to prop you up. Move down. Push . . . Not the footboard, the baby. That's right. Whoa . . . lookie there! He's as long as his daddy. Push, Cora. Yell all you want, but keep pushing. Don't hold back. Two little fellas. Wow!"

Ruth stirs. The word is out. Even the stars listen as her brothers' cries join the night chorus. Mother Nature is bragging about her shining accomplishment.

I feel part of something magical.

An hour later Ruthie and the yellow kitty are in bed. Two sticky, froggy little boys have been washed—one by me—and wrapped, with Dr. Nesbitt's shoelaces secured around their belly buttons.

We clean up and pack up. Dr. Nesbitt pads to the car in his stocking feet and nudges it into reverse. Two little kerosene lamp flames in the window of Ruthie's house greet the first rays of morning.

Something is new inside me too. But it's still too close to sort out. I only know I could stay awake forever.

Dr. Nesbitt sighs and whacks the seat. "Damn it!"

"What? Dr. Nesbitt?"

"Never once, in my whole practice life, have I ever forgotten my cord clamps. They're totally useless sitting on the counter in my office." He glances over at the grin on my face.

"Your shoelaces worked perfectly," I say. "I don't think those babies knew the difference." Our headlights create a tunnel in the mist. "Well, a lot of help I was," I say. "Think how many times you and Ellis had to step over me!"

"My pleasure, Iris. A bit unconventional . . . but you knew exactly what you were doing. Thanks to you, Cora stopped worrying about Ruthie and concentrated on those boys."

I sit straighter on the seat. "I'd like to bake a cobbler and check in on them this afternoon. I could take Mrs. Nesbitt. She'd like that."

Dr. Nesbitt gives me a respectful little nod and smiles. "Might you let me come along, too?"

"My pleasure," I say, as the stars tuck themselves into the dawn.

CHAPTER 15

August 12, 1926

Dearest Iris,

Your father was tinkering with our new cash register this morning when he threw up his arms and exclaimed, "Celeste, write Iris. We need another hand around here!" So . . . c'est moi! He said you're a whiz at punching keys. Hopefully they'll be flying in September with the mountain of sales we expect. Hope you're ready for hard work.

We are exhausted but elated! The grand opening simply

sparkled. I've enclosed the new Bootery business card. Every day we learn more about our Kansas City customers—demanding and discerning, to say the least. Sound like anyone else you know???

No nibbles on the Atchison house. If I had half a minute I'd come up there and put a polish on the place. The first impression—that front porch—cries out for a scrub and fresh paint. Actually the whole place needs . . . something! Your father suggested you send a list—hopefully short—of what you want to keep.

We signed a two-year lease at the Del Mar Apartments. You will love it! It's on the fourth floor—two bedrooms, a railed balcony, a full kitchen, and a southern exposure. I can't wait to display my whatnots and wedding gifts in the light of day. I do hope you're better about dusting than I am!

Charles plans a trip to Atchison next week to arrange the shipping of his desk, the wardrobe, and bookcases. We won't have a corner to squeeze in that piano. Too bad and too too too many details for my rattled brain! Your father is ecstatic to move out of his rooming house. My motto is: Petite is perfect for feet, but not living quarters!

Just the same, we decided it's best for you to live

with me until Oct 10th, even though my apartment's no bigger than a shoe box. (We'll be just like sisters.) It'll be a pinch, but who has time to spend there anyhoo?

Have you made a decision about high school? I understand you already have the credentials to graduate! Inherited your father's brains, didn't you? If a senior year is not necessary, we hope you will finish your education on Petticoat Lane just like I did. Lots of young girls, with the right touch, can work their way up from stockroom to salesperson to model!

I don't know the nature of your connection with the Nesbitts, but if you wish, please invite them to the nuptials. I doubt the elderly mother could come, but it's the proper thing to do, unless you think they'd feel out of place. My land, what an experience you've had in Wellsford. We're dying to hear all your folksy farm stories.

Enough of my rambling. Less than a month until Labor Day and your debut in Kansas City.

Au revoir!
X O X O
Celeste "Baldwin" –to–be!!

I drop the letter on the table, grab the sides of my head, then wipe my fingers on my skirt as though Celeste's personality has rubbed off on them. I flip the pages to the blank side, grab Mrs. Nesbitt's crossword pencil, and scribble a reply:

Dearest Celeste,

Here's my list. It's not things, it's advice for living with my father.

1. Project yourself! Wear bright colors, strong perfume, and heels that click. Otherwise he will forget you are there.

2. Don't cough. He'll be mad that you have tuberculosis.

3. Remember your shoes are more important to him than your eyes.

4. Learn to drive yourself.

5. Advertise your upcoming birthday, or else you will buy, wrap, and open your own presents.

6. Find a friend who will listen to you. That person is not me.

7. If you need to know something, read his mail.

8. Pretend you are a virgin no matter what.

9. Collect thousands of exclamation points inside you—you will need them to stay excited about him!!!!

10. Get rid of your question marks??? He will not answer your questions.

11. He'll expect two sugar lumps in his coffee. He will not remember if you drink coffee.

12. Don't tell him about this advice. He hates anything cheap, much less free!

P.S. For more luck, spit on a horseshoe and lick the hind leg of a white mule every day. Avoid whistling in graveyards and cross-eyed people.

P.P.S. I am bringing my chickens to live with us. More folksy advice: If you swallow a raw chicken heart on your wedding day, it'll bring good luck in love.

I slump at the kitchen table, shake out my writing hand. My heart sinks. For a strange moment I truly want to protect Celeste from the future with him. She's counting on so much, and she wants me to be happy for her, *with* her.

The ghosts crowding my cellar and all the goddesses know about Daddy by now. So do Carl and Leroy. But the Nesbitts don't. They don't know I am nothing to him. Celeste will find out she's nothing too. I wonder if Mama knew. Did she get gritty and ground up inside every time he opened his mouth? Did she ever dig in the heels of her Baldwin's boots?

I hear Henry scraping across Mrs. Nesbitt's floor. She's up from her nap.

I fold the two-faced letter that I won't mail to Celeste. But I could leave it right here on the table for Mrs. Nesbitt to find. She's curious and meddlesome enough to read it, at least until Gladys Dilgert arrives full of blabber about *her* storybook family.

I know how Mrs. Nesbitt would answer the question: Does Iris ever tell stories about her mama and daddy?

Never.

Marie and I carry the letter to my room, put my brilliant advice and Celeste's enthusiasm about her whatnots in my Kotex drawer.

Marie curls up on my coverlet, then sits up suddenly, perks her ears. I hear the knock. She hops from the bed and races to the front door, barking her head off. I wipe my eyes, cold fear zipping through me. Who else could it be but Cecil, with his habit of showing up when Dr. Nesbitt's gone?

I walk into the hall wishing I had the shotgun, even though I know nothing about using it. Why is he at the *front* door? I pull back the sheers. Neither Cecil's wagon nor his car is in the driveway.

Marie is fit to be tied, frantically circling the front hall. Mrs. Nesbitt and Henry tap up behind me. I open the door and squint at a man. He's broad-shouldered, his arms and neck suntanned, his face shadowed beneath a hat.

Marie darts out, sniffs his scuffed work boots and knapsack.

A flame of rust-colored hair catches the sun when he removes his hat. He looks down in my eyes, his face deadly serious.

"Leroy!"

CHAPTER 16

He stays planted on the stoop, looking from me to Mrs. Nesbitt and back. "Have you gotten the telegram?"

I shake my head. Mrs. Nesbitt grips Henry in both hands.

"It's your dad." Leroy's eyes match Mrs. Nesbitt's jade earrings. "He was in his car. He got hit . . . by a train." Leroy shakes his head, his eyes bolted to mine.

"Where is he?" I ask.

I watch crows quietly collect on the telephone wire behind Leroy. Marie pads across the carpet runner and sits by Henry. Even my cellar ghosts are silent.

Leroy's voice is husky and soft. "He didn't beat the train, Iris."

"Was he alone?" Mrs. Nesbitt asks softly.

"Yes, ma'am."

Mrs. Nesbitt leads us into the front room. I think of the day I arrived, perched on the divan, sure that Mrs. Nesbitt was dead. It's still terrible in here, dust-choked and dark. Mrs. Nesbitt must feel it too. She and Leroy raise the shades, open the stuck windows. They pull chairs up to the sofa so we form a little ring.

"I was delivering ice to the rail crew when they got the news," Leroy explains. "It happened late this morning. He was outside Atchison, coming over from Kansas City."

I picture the pages of advice for Celeste I just tucked away in my bottom drawer. It seems a hundred years ago. I try to remember the last time my father wrote me himself. Did I save the letter? Where's my picture of him?

I re-create the accident in my mind. I see Daddy's shiny new Cadillac racing down the road toward Atchison, a tornado of dust in his wake. I hear the engine grind and the flap of his shirtsleeves in the open window. He eyes the approaching train and speeds up. I hear the long frantic train whistle, the slashing and screeching.

A wall comes in my mind. I realize I've been holding my breath.

I remember that nice little paper doll family on the train and the peppermint they gave me. After a long moment I ask, "Was it a freight train or a passenger train?"

"What?"

"That hit Daddy."

"Passenger . . ." Leroy says.

"Was anybody on the train hurt?"

"I don't know. I hitchhiked here the minute I heard."

I remember the squealing brakes and lurch when we hit that hobo. I hear the frantic barking of his dog before she arrived here and became Marie. Their nice little hobo family of two was broken up just like mine.

Mrs. Nesbitt excuses herself to call Avery. Marie follows her out.

Leroy and I stare at the piano across the room and the shrouded painting above it. I say, "Do you remember Mrs. Andrews' husband before he died? He was so . . ."

Leroy nods. "Tired."

"The end of his old life crept up on him. So did the end of Mama's young life. Sickness. They knew it was coming." I look up at Leroy. He looks right back. "What was Daddy racing this time? Himself?"

We watch dust twirl as though we've shaken it from a long, dull dream. "Mrs. Nesbitt keeps this room in memory of her son who was killed. She still loves him so much." I sit silent a long moment. "A moth could fly right through me, Leroy. I don't feel anything."

Leroy plays with a divan pillow. Lifting all that ice and being in the sun have made him look like his old self plus someone new. But his voice and eyes are the same. So is the way he turns his feet in and rests his arms across his knees when he sits.

"It was fine of you to come here and tell Iris in person," Dr. Nesbitt says when he gets home. He claps Leroy on the back. Everybody helps me make dinner. Mrs. Nesbitt insists on setting the table. Dr. Nesbitt bastes the roast chicken, then stirs and seasons the lima beans. Leroy chops sweet potatoes and sprinkles them with butter and brown sugar. We eat and eat. When the telegram arrives, Dr. Nesbitt answers the door. I nod for him to go ahead and read it to himself. After a moment he folds it back in the yellow Western Union envelope, gives it to me, then clasps the paper and my hands in his. I notice how long and clean and smooth his fingernails are despite all the human bodies—dead and alive—they have touched.

The conversation spinning between Leroy and the Nesbitts is like a bowl I can just float in tonight. But I feel their eyes on me, in case I start to drown.

It's dark with a sliver of moon. Leroy and I sit on the bench in the yard long after dinner.

"You wanna talk?" he asks.

"Not now."

"Okay." Leroy bends down to Marie. "How about you, girl?"

We stroke her back with our bare feet. "It's stupid. I don't ever come out here at night," I say, looking up. The longer we look, the more stars come out. "Why do you think they chained them up into constellations? All those animals and Greek gods. Outside of Orion and the Big and Little Dippers, I can't make out any of them."

Leroy clasps his hands behind his head. I hear him stretch. He smells of soap and shaving cream. "Me neither." He points into the infinite twinkling net. "What about the dim, gold ones?"

"They're orphan stars, not part of constellations."

"Hmmm . . ."

"They need dusting."

"Dusting?"

"And polishing. Here. See?" I reach up, capture one in my hand and rub it against Leroy's cheek. His skin is soft and close. It's so dark I can't tell the look on his face, but I hear his breathing change.

"I'm so sorry, Iris . . . It's . . ."

"You can tell me all that tomorrow."

"Okay." He releases a long breath. "It looks like the stars are moving instead of us."

"They're hobos sailing home."

"That's nice."

The house sparkles. Dr. Nesbitt has lit lamps in the parlor. Through the window we see him shaking out sheets, fluffing a pillow. He's concocting a sleeping pallet for Leroy. No doubt it will be as tight and crisp as a hospital bed.

I take Leroy's hand in the same way I hold Mrs. Nesbitt's. It's callused and strong. I push my thumbs into his broad palm. I lock my fingers with his, then pull them away. Dr. Nesbitt's voice carries from the house. He's talking to someone on the telephone.

Leroy pulls me up. "Let's get out from under these branches, where we can see the sky better." We step our way over curved, bare tree roots and onto the lawn.

There's a steady sweep of breeze that smells like warm land and moonlight. We sit and look up. Without a word Leroy reaches over, gently feels for my bone hairpin and just pulls it out. My hair flops down my back in a long lazy knot. He leans back on his elbows. "The clouds look like shreds of the Milky Way."

"Or lace on midnight blue velvet." I lie on my back. The damp grass spreading in every direction soaks through my dress. "I am *on* earth. Not buried."

"Right, Iris."

Leroy lies down, slides his arms around me.

"This okay?" he asks.

I can't think, can't speak over the blood noise in my ears.

"Tell me to move away," he says deep in my ear.

I reach my arm around his side. "Move away, Leroy," I say in a voice not my own.

"No."

He moves closer, presses the small of my back. The full length of him is against the full length of me. We're chained. An earthly constellation of two.

"I take it back about not feeling anything," I say.

We lock our feet. Breathe together, Leroy's heart on mine.

The feeling sweeps through my breasts, down my legs and spine, deep into the root of me, and out my fingertips.

We've arrived somewhere new.

The rhythm of a faraway train rocks the field mice and Orion and Ruthie's baby brothers. I am just like them, I think, a night creature pressed hard against life.

CHAPTER 17

All night long the goddesses guard me from my ghosts.

Tuesday I wake up to the smell of coffee and Leroy's easy laugh coming from the kitchen. Patches of sun shuffle across the rug. I stretch, roll to my side, and reach out, back in the moonlit grass floating up and up.

The phone rings. I hear Dr. Nesbitt say, "Celeste," and "Yes, I'll tell her."

I wash my face, sprinkle powder under my dress, and walk down the hall barefoot.

When I come in the kitchen Dr. and Mrs. Nesbitt don't do any of the things I would hate. They don't stop talking. They don't tilt their long faces and pat me on the shoulder, sorry that I'm not part of their club for folks who understand God's whim. No one explains that for some mysterious reason He needed the last of my family to get smashed by a train.

In fact, Leroy looks up at me, like he's still gazing at a star. I see my hairpin in his pants pocket. He puts his hand over it—his way of saying he's not giving it back.

Dr. Nesbitt stands at the stove. "I told Leroy that today, *I* wear the apron in the family. Do you want bacon and eggs, Iris?"

Marie's stumpy tail taps the linoleum at the word bacon. She gives me a pleading look.

"Yes, thank you."

Mrs. Nesbitt sparkles, a ruby in her fiery Japanese jacket and slippers. Leroy straddles his chair. His pale blue shirtsleeves are rolled back. He looks as if he could reach over and lift Mrs. Nesbitt and her chair in one hand. I straighten my back. Have I changed that much too?

We discuss how everybody slept and how Leroy needs a tour of the chicken house. I glance at the telephone on a triangle-shaped table in the corner. "I have got to call Celeste back," I say flatly. "She's tried to reach me, hasn't she?"

"Twice," Dr. Nesbitt says.

It takes forever for the operator to make the connection. I haven't given a thought about what to expect or what to say.

"Iris?"

"Celeste."

There's silence. I cautiously step onto the gaping, rickety bridge that connects us: my father. "I'm so . . ."

Celeste interrupts, her voice panicky, bossy. "We'll sit together at the service. We're a family now."

No.

I focus on my group still rooted around the breakfast table. Dr. Nesbitt lowers his coffee cup. Leroy doodles on Mrs. Nesbitt's crossword. I know they can hear Celeste's every word.

She sniffs and whines. "I wanted you to catch the bouquet."

"Bouquet?"

"At my *wedding*! Oh, God. Everything . . . I'm . . . except . . ." Celeste dissolves into sobs.

Mrs. Nesbitt hands me her hankie. Leroy shakes his head.

"You need to come to Kansas City right now," Celeste pleads. "Please."

"Don't you mean Atchison? I thought the funeral would be in . . ."

"You've got to move before our Labor Day weekend sale, Iris. You're good with numbers, and we've got so much to do at the store."

I start coughing. Celeste has sucked my breath right through the phone.

Her voice gets wobbly. "My sister promised to come from Oklahoma! I wanted her to see my store, our new apartment. Of course, she already has a rich husband and three *perfect* children." Celeste's tone becomes confidential. "But so what? She's lost her figure and she's only twenty-six!"

"She's coming for the memorial?"

"No! The wedding."

"But . . ."

"Please, Iris . . ."

There's a long impossible pause. I imagine every ear between Wellsford and Kansas City listening on the party line.

"I'll call you back," I say.

"Iris. Please come. You know your daddy would want you to."

"I'll call."

I hang up. Marie looks up at me. I toss her a bite of bacon. Mrs. Nesbitt folds her hands. Dr. Nesbitt pours more coffee. I take a long sip, let the steam fill my nose. "God! Celeste is . . ." I shudder. "Mixed up. I need to call Carl about the arrangements before she does."

Leroy explains Carl to the Nesbitts. They help me think through Daddy's funeral details. I decide I don't want a visitation like Mama had. We can't get the house ready for it. The services will be Thursday at the church in Atchison with another at the cemetery.

Mrs. Nesbitt holds my hand while I call Carl. "Yes, I know you are. . . . Thank you. Could you please call Reverend Wolver for me? Set the service for Thursday afternoon? And, Carl, would you pick out a casket? It needs to be the glossiest black they have, with polished silver handles . . . and expensive."

Leroy smiles.

"You know exactly what I mean. Nothing cheap."

We hang up with the promise to talk again this afternoon.

I pace the kitchen. Celeste's dizzy desperation shoves at me all the way from Kansas City. I imagine us bumping around her little apartment together. A wall, not a bridge, grows inside. I erupt to the group at the table. "Celeste was all dolled up to marry my father and give birth to a shoe store. That's all the family they wanted . . . not *me*. What am I supposed to do with her? I'm not her housekeeper, or her bookkeeper, or her sister, either. She's already got a living, breathing sister, even if all they do is *project* their two-faced perfectly phony selves at each other!"

The Nesbitts' stunned looks make me feel like I just spit on everybody, including Daddy. I burst into tears and out the door.

Leroy follows me to the stinky chicken house. "I'm gonna move in here," I sputter. "There's room for one more chicken."

Leroy stuffs his hands in his pockets. "Why can't you stay out here with them?"

"Because they need somebody to *help* them instead of a hateful, crazy person who is only good at hurling raw eggs."

Leroy screws up his face. *"What?"*

"Never mind, Leroy. The Nesbitts didn't know much about Daddy or Celeste . . . until now. They probably thought that they were . . . well, they probably wondered what he was like, because I never . . . But, anyway, they haven't offered, and they've hired somebody else." I roll my eyes. "Gladys Dilgert. So, la-di-da. Here she comes . . . and there I go."

"So? Have Gladys go live with Celeste and you stay here."

Leroy sneezes. The chickens fuss and peck. "You're making them nervous, Leroy." I grab the basket and gather eggs—so wound up I could break one in my fist.

I hear footsteps crunch across the driveway. "Iris?" Dr. and Mrs. Nesbitt gingerly step in, fanning their faces. I turn to them, blinking in the dusty light. Dr. Nesbitt still wears the red-and-white checked apron. "Does your father have a will?" he asks.

"Sir?"

"A will."

"I suppose so."

"Would he have changed it yet, to include Celeste?"

"I don't know."

Mrs. Nesbitt covers her nose with her hankie. I worry about her satin slippers in the chicken manure.

"Does he have any living relatives besides you?"

"No, sir. His brother, Marion, died."

"Do you plan to go to Atchison tomorrow?"

"Yes. I need to check the train." I hear the phone ringing in the house. Celeste.

Dr. Nesbitt says firmly, "We know Leroy has to leave today. Mother and I would like to drive you to Atchison tomorrow, stay overnight, and go to the services on Thursday. In fact, Mother can stay longer, to help you sort through what needs doing at your house."

"Thank you." My mind reels. "I guess I should pack everything. My trunk . . ."

Mrs. Nesbitt's voice is solemn, official. "Iris, our contract with you goes through Labor Day, so you will be unavailable to Celeste until then. I trust you will tell her as much."

Leroy and I sit on the stoop. I shiver in the August heat. "I think Celeste gave me permanent poison ivy."

He moves close, rubs my arms. "Here, give me the poison ivy. I'll get rid of it for you." He cups my hands. I feel the pulse in his thumbs and wrists.

"Sit next to me," I say.

"I am."

"On Thursday."

"Okay."

We take Leroy to the depot. "We can all stay at my house in Atchison, although it will be kinda musty," I tell Mrs. Nesbitt on the way back.

"And dusty," she adds. "Don't worry about that now, you've got enough on your mind."

"I guess Daddy will be buried by Mama . . ."

Tears well up. I blot them on my sleeve and try to remember the two of them together in their living lives. I have only one memory of it, on the porch at the sanatorium. Daddy sits in a rocker, reading Mama a letter.

She has her eyes shut, but you can tell she's listening. His head is bent, the afternoon sunlight making his hair look silver, then black, then silver as he rocks. I wonder who wrote that letter. A friend maybe? Did she write back? What would she have said? Was she strong or funny or snooty or kind? Was she fumbly like me? Was she good with numbers?

What will she do with Daddy when he shows up in heaven?

CHAPTER 18

Under a bruised sky, fingers of wind stroke the wheat from bleached gold to tan and back. We pass threshing machines crouched under showers of dust and straw. Fat hay bales dot the landscape.

I'm in the backseat, wondering if the sky will cry and turn the roads to mud before we get to Atchison. The shifting wheat makes the land look upholstered in suede. I shut my eyes, recalling our store and Carl at his bench in the back room.

"Charles, you tryin' to make my life miserable, sellin' this suede? Why every spit of grease and horse shit in Atchison, Kansas, just falls in love with it."

Suede.

Daddy's shoes!

I sit straight. Oh, God. Oh, no! I didn't tell Carl to pick out shoes. Daddy can't go anywhere without the right footwear.

"Dr. Nesbitt!" I say. "We need to head straight for Daddy's store when we get to Atchison. It's real important."

Mrs. Nesbitt turns with a curious expression. "Dear?"

I stutter about reverse leather and fashion and Daddy's holy attitude toward the proper shoes for every occasion—even walking through the Valley of the Shadow.

"So your father was a smart dresser, I gather."

I nod, sick with forgetting the one thing I *can* do for him now, the one thing I ever truly understood about him.

Dr. Nesbitt accelerates a bit. He must feel the engine burning in me to resolve what other folks would find a silly detail at a time like this. But my father was a detail man in every way except one—the details of me.

In the distance ahead I see a railroad crossing with a faded sign. But there is no train today.

Morbid takes over. I sit back, wondering what shoes Daddy was wearing when he died. A sickening image of them scuffed and crushed comes to my mind.

How did the engineer feel closing in on that crossing, unable to stop, his warnings ignored? How must he be feeling now, living with that horrid jolt in his bones? And what of the passengers trapped on the train, knocked and bruised by the impact?

A wall inside me crumbles. In my mind I see the look of

gritty determination on my father's face—the expression I saw when riding with him on a road much like this one years ago, the time he almost killed us trying to beat a freight train.

Dark feelings rush in. I turn clammy, lean forward, grip the top of the front seat, panicked.

"Dr. Nesbitt! Stop at the crossing—*please!*"

We roll up to a rusty sign squeaking in the wind. Dr. Nesbitt hits the brake and turns the engine off.

Dust settles around our car. I sit with my hands over my face. My worst memory has leaped over the barrier inside. I am eight years old again, trapped in the car with my father.

The ground rumbles beneath us. Out my window I see the locomotive bearing down, its whistle shrieking one warning after another: *STOP! Get out of the way!* But Daddy, with me right beside him, speeds up and shoots straight for the crossing, his hands gripping on the steering wheel, his shirtsleeves billowing in the wind.

The train can't stop for us, and Daddy won't stop for it. A wild black ghost of exhaust tumbles backward over the open coal cars.

Daddy's teeth are gritted, his jaw working.

NO! NO! I grab the door handle, squeeze my eyes shut, every part of me screaming *STOP!* but my mouth.

The slashing beat of the train sounds like knife blades sharpened against the rails. We fly through gravel, *whack-whack* over the tracks, then stop sharp. I knock forward, hit my hands on the dash. My knees bang the floor. The hulking wall of train bursts through our car dust and disappears.

Everything is deathly quiet.

Dizzy, panting, I watch pinpoints of blood appear on my skinned knees. Daddy smoothes his hair. Sweat glistens on his forehead. My hands are ice.

He takes a deep breath, looks over at me, his wide eyes almost mocking. He throws his arm nonchalantly over the seat back. "See, Iris? We had all the time in the world."

We did not. You almost killed us.

Rage and fear boil in me.

Why did you do that?

He tilts his head, gives me a half smile, then gets back to the business of Sunday driving, wheeling along as though my terror counts for less than the squished bugs on his windshield.

Now I huddle in the back of the Nesbitts' car, panting into the palms of my hands. I know they are watching me, but they do not say a word. My hands tingle. I taste blood. I've bitten my lip.

How can a memory feel so *alive*? How can Daddy be *dead*?

I wrap myself in my arms, my heart stalled as it was then—the first time I really knew I couldn't trust him, the first of many times I tasted the fear of losing him.

And now I have.

We did *not* have all the time in the world.

I look up, watch thunderheads tumble over the horizon. Fat raindrops hit Dr. Nesbitt's windshield, pulling the dust into muddy tears. The tracks are empty. The only train today was the one streaking back to that horrible memory.

Dr. Nesbitt checks me in the mirror. "Are you all right?" he says softly. But I can't answer.

After a long moment I speak to the backs of their heads. "I have an awful memory from when I was little. My father almost killed himself—and me—trying to beat a train at a crossing like this one."

"Was it this very spot?" Mrs. Nesbitt asks.

"No, we were heading toward Kansas City on a Sunday drive that day. I haven't been past it since. But nothing was right with us after that. Maybe before that. I don't know."

They nod, tilting their heads in exactly the same way.

I look down the tracks—right, left. Then repeat. I listen to the hollow wind. "We can go now," I whisper. "Thank you for stopping for me."

We arrive in Atchison in the early afternoon. I direct Dr. Nesbitt to Daddy's store. The Nesbitts meet Carl and get a tour of the back room while I pick out the shoes. The store smells of shoe polish and leather glue. I rub the edge of the worn oak countertop under Daddy's beloved cash register, bounce his scratched glass paperweight in the palm of my hand. On the surface everything is in perfect order.

My father's world.

I wonder what the Kansas City store smells like—probably Celeste's perfume.

Carl looks so sad and sorry. He packages Daddy's shoes, gives me a hug.

We drive on to the mortuary. The funeral director

greets us at the door, motions us to a stiff purple divan in the hall, and walks away. I sit between the Nesbitts, feeling like ten different people wrapped into one.

Voices and footsteps echo from rooms down the long corridor. I fold Mrs. Nesbitt's hand inside mine, careful not to crush her fingers. My other hand steadies the shoe box on my lap.

The director returns and ushers us to a dim room with my father's coffin on a curtained table. It's huge and slick, with curvy silver trim and bulky handles. There are sprays of lilies and roses on top and a florist-shop wreath on a spindly wire stand.

I have never seen my father wear shoes when he's lying down, except his slippers. He would just never do that. I picture him upright, chatting with customers, guiding them by the elbow through his store, smiling his salesman smile. I see him wearing these shiny coffin shoes walking in Kansas City with Celeste hooked to his arm.

God... I squeeze my eyes. *What's wrong with me?*

"Why's the lid closed?" I ask the mortician, handing him the shoe box.

He shakes his head. "The accident, Miss Baldwin. We'll take care of your wishes with these as best we can. God bless you."

While Leroy shows Dr. Nesbitt around Atchison, Mrs. Nesbitt and I go home. Mrs. Andrews has opened the parlor windows and swept the front porch. Thanks to her, there are fresh sheets for us tonight and supper—pot roast, biscuits, pickled beets, and peanut brittle.

While Mrs. Nesbitt naps on a twin bed in my room, I sit on the edge of the divan, avoiding thoughts about the FOR SALE sign in the front yard. I know what's coming. In a moment I'll start chopping everything—the lampshades, doorknobs, photos, even Mama's old secretary desk—into a thousand morbid memories.

I half expect the hands on our mantel clock to move backward. The next-door neighbor has mowed over a bunch of chives in his side yard. The oniony smell drifts in, shifting my mind to Wellsford. I'm dusting with Mrs. Nesbitt, cherishing every inch of her precious jasmine bedroom. I hear the chickens and cows and Marie's constant commentary of barks and greetings and growls. I feel the heaven of Leroy's body under that roof of stars. I see the fountain pen and letter holder on Dr. Nesbitt's desk.

I shake my head. There is nothing on Daddy's desk today but a fine layer of dust.

His bedroom door is shut. I make myself go in and raise the blinds. My hands fly to my chest. Facing me on the floor, in a shaft of late afternoon light, are his old leather slippers, looking as though they have just stepped out of the wardrobe. I stare at the one pair of his shoes that hold the history of our life here together. They are polished, of course, but the creases and shape are so much my father, I see his weight still on them, feel him standing there. Barely breathing, I step forward.

"Daddy?" I whisper to the space above the slippers.

Yes, Iris.

"Are you all right?"

Yes.

"Where are you?"

I don't know.

I'm trembling, hopeful that maybe he'll explain what happened, knowing he won't. "Were you trying to beat the train again, or was it an accident?"

No reply.

Tears roll down my face. I take a deep breath, wondering why it is always so empty between us. Without expecting to, I ask, "Is Mama there?"

Silence.

I imagine the smooth wall of his cheek, how he turned his face away whenever I mentioned her. I glance around his bedroom, cleared of the everyday belongings he took to his apartment in Kansas City. *Kansas City.* I step back. "Wh . . . what about me? Celeste says I should live with her now."

Instead of words, I get an image of Celeste married to someone else. I'm not in the picture.

I step forward. "I *said*, 'what about me'?"

I'm thinking.

I stare at thin air. "You never could answer that one, Daddy."

You'd never trust my answer even if I had one, Iris.

"But . . ." I pause, watch the sun wash his slippers. "I guess you're right. That is *one* thing you *do* know about me."

I feel something tiny but new—that bit of honesty—even if it's just me talking to myself. I sniff the cedar lining of his wardrobe, count his collection of agate marbles in a box on the dresser. It's time to cry again, but I don't. I unlace my boots, remove my socks, and stand, twisting my bare feet on the scratchy wool rug. I walk up to his slippers. I study their shiny brown outsides, then walk around and slip into them the way I did as a little girl.

Tears streaming, I wriggle my toes, still trying to somehow absorb his footprint.

I'm awake half the night. It's strange having Dr. Nesbitt asleep in Daddy's bed. The feel of the creases Mrs. Andrews's ironing left in my sheets, the crisscross call of Atchison train whistles, the electric yard-light next door, and Mrs. Nesbitt's soft snoring combine—two worlds mixed.

Very soon I will not be at home in either one.

Thursday afternoon the church smells like coffee and gingerbread, made by the circle ladies for Daddy's reception after the service and burial. Reverend Wolver welcomes everybody at the door—community people, Carl, Mrs. Andrews, Leroy's parents, and Daddy's store employees. But he has forgotten my name. He looks ancient and smells like overcooked turnips.

Celeste is here, but her sister didn't come. Neither did her friends. Her face resembles a wet hankie smeared with lipstick. She sits next to me on the pew, squeezing the life-blood out of my right hand.

Leroy is on my left, then the Nesbitts. Leroy and I barely touch, but we breathe together—a secret hymn pumping between us.

Reverend Wolver's service is not about my father. It's not about any of us, really. The homily sounds like he's chewing a piece of gristle. I look out the window at an empty bird feeder. Forget his Psalms and prayers. Forget the forgiveness of our infinite sins. What we need is a list of advice for living *without* Charles Baldwin.

Who will I be mad at?

What will I feed my ghosts?

How will Celeste and I fill the future?

We sit in folding chairs at the cemetery. Daddy's elegant casket reminds me of a tuxedo. The dark tarp surrounding the coffin hole covers Mama's headstone. I have no recollection of her service here.

Celeste's gardenia perfume mixes with the musty black dirt. She dabs her eyes and glances at the funeral car. She wants out of here. I don't blame her. She's too young for endings. I'm sure she figures if Charles Baldwin can't be her partner in Kansas City, then he's better off in Atchison.

As they lower the box, I imagine the long, sooty trail of a train whistle—ashes to ashes, dust to dust. I cannot cry. I can't pray for Daddy's departed soul. The only thing to do is breathe, feed air to my heart.

"Dead people never sleep," Celeste whispers when we're back at the church. "That's why they keep you awake at night. The deceased are not on a regular schedule." She glances around the room. I wonder if she's scouting for Daddy's ghost. "Oh, I know I sound nuts." She shivers. "But I haven't slept since Monday. I guess it shows. I'm so alone now." She scrunches her face to fight off tears. "Charles and I just adored Kansas City, and that store, and . . ."

I cut her off, force the sentence before I chicken out: "I have a contract with the Nesbitts, Celeste, and I cannot move until after Labor Day."

Her tone becomes suddenly businesslike. "The Tuesday after, then." She raises her arms heavenward, offering God her sermon. "I had to give up my wedding dress, my monogrammed towels, and our new apartment. I have nowhere for all the gifts. Nobody. The store was *everything*." She gives me a soulful look. "You simply can't imagine what it's like, Iris."

Mrs. Nesbitt, as usual, has not missed a thing. She holds me—and Celeste—in her strong gaze. What dawns on me is something Mrs. Nesbitt has seen too: Celeste is just a hobo in stockings and pearls.

We drive her to the station a bit early. She is anxious to get going, she says, there's so much to do, no time to go to my house now. With a bright smile she reminds me how "thrilled your daddy must be knowing you plan to live with me and help run the Bootery." She swoops up the train steps, turning her ankle in the process. But she doesn't stop, doesn't look back.

"I hope she sleeps on the trip," Mrs. Nesbitt says as she waves at the caboose.

CHAPTER 19

All the signs point at each other.
I somersault in muddy water.
We trip on the tracks.
Mama's crying.
Money burns.
I'm falling.

I sit on our porch swing, let its squeak grind my dream fragments away. It's early Friday morning and I have already made a mistake. I have awakened a spider. My rocking has shredded her lacy home, spun overnight between the ceiling and the swing chains. I miss Marie, her yipping enthusiasm at the beginning of every day. I miss the way my fussy chicks need me at dawn. I'm glad we voted for one of Dr. Nesbitt's patients to feed them while we're gone, not Cecil . . . or Dot.

I sat out here, just like this, on the afternoon of Mama's funeral visitation. Just six-year-old me with a piece of chocolate cake on a blue-flowered plate, and the cold, boney-white November sky. My fancy church shoes didn't reach the floor, so I couldn't push off to swing. I remember scooting to the edge and scraping them back and forth across the cement floor until the toes were scuffed the color of chalk.

This morning the FOR SALE sign in the front yard looks crippled, with grass tufted around its bent stake. A wall builds between me and the day ahead—a whirlpool of impossible decisions and undoings. Everything will need selling, or moving, or rearranging. But there's no right place for any of it, including the most awkward piece of furniture: me. I'm too empty to sell. I'm too replaceable to stay in Wellsford, and I'm too big for Celeste's apartment.

Mrs. Nesbitt and Henry come out. I help her onto the swing. She's light as a feather in her ivory silk robe.

She points to the yard, squints. "Do you find that sign . . . distracting?"

I wipe my eyes. "It's horrible." I rattle off the swing, rock the pole out of the dirt, and put the sign facedown in the side yard.

"There. Now we can think more clearly," Mrs. Nesbitt remarks. "How'd you sleep?"

I shut my eyes. "I was busy all night being morbid—drowning and tripping. I swear, I could cry at a broken toothpick this morning."

"Did you dream you were naked in a hailstorm?" she asks. "Did you get hit by a rolling snake?"

I half smile. "I'll save those for tonight."

Someone next door has started cooking sausage. Squirrels skitter across our picket fence. "I ruined her web," I say, pointing to an elegant black spider hanging above us. Her legs are drawn in. She looks like a mighty little upside-down cage.

Mrs. Nesbitt studies the spider a long moment. "She's protecting herself," Mrs. Nesbitt says, "but you wait; spiders are industrious. They take care of what's theirs. Once she copes with losing her web, she'll open up and weave another one."

We move in rhythm with the rusty chains. Although it's early, the locusts start their loud singsong chant. "Our squealing must have inspired them," Mrs. Nesbitt says above the noise.

"I can't oil the locusts, but I can stop the squeak." I go inside, return with a little oil can and a rag.

"There! Good for you. You did something unmorbid," Mrs. Nesbitt says. "Better than I would have done under the circumstances."

I raise the tiny can to her. "This swing has needed oiling my whole life."

She smiles.

Before I lose the strength of the moment, I add, "I spoke with Daddy yesterday."

Mrs. Nesbitt registers the meaning of my remark, holds me in a long look and nods. "That was brave."

I smile. "Yep."

Dr. Nesbitt steps outside with a cup of coffee. "How are you, ladies?"

Mrs. Nesbitt taps her fists together. "Moving forward . . . one link at a time."

Dr. Nesbitt sits on the porch step. He's already dressed for the day, one of the few he has spent without seeing patients in a long while. "Mother and I were talking yesterday, Iris. I plan to drive home today after we see your father's attorney. You and Mother call me when you're ready to come home. I suspect it'll be a full car."

Mrs. Nesbitt turns to me. Her tone is serious. "I told Avery that we have lots of dusting to do here. It simply can't be rushed."

In the afternoon we consult Daddy's lawyer about his last will and testament. We learn that he planned to leave the Bootery in Kansas City to Celeste Simmons Baldwin and everything else to me. "A curious decision," the attorney says, "the way it's divided up. But . . . it's of no consequence." He slides the document across his desk. "It has not been signed and witnessed."

"So there is no will?" I ask.

"Your father's *earlier* will, written after your mother's death, still stands." He gives me a deep look. "You are the sole beneficiary of both stores, the house, all the property, all the assets. Since your father and Miss Simmons were unmarried at the time of his demise, you have no obligation to her whatsoever."

I sense the lawyer has met Celeste. I imagine the attorney detected a sour petal in Mrs. Baldwin-to-be's Jungle Gardenia perfume. "Does Celeste know it was not signed?" I ask.

"Yes. Your father planned to take care of it during his"— he looks down—"ill-fated trip to Atchison." He turns to Dr. and Mrs. Nesbitt. "Until the age of eighteen, Iris will need both a legal guardian and a conservator of her estate. Someone trustworthy must be assigned to manage her assets and help with her life decisions. I imagine Celeste Simmons wants very much to be that individual."

I look up at the Nesbitts, but they stare at the wood grain tabletop as though I've already moved to Kansas City.

They don't talk all the way home. My heart wilts. My bad dreams have come true. I am tripping right into the muddy water rising around the former Mrs. Charles Baldwin-to-be.

Dr. Nesbitt loads his grip in the car. "If you don't mind a bit of advice, Iris, I'd keep the will quiet until you get your head above water. I'm going to stop by the store, tell Carl goodbye." We wave from the porch as he drives off with the file on the seat.

The phone rings inside. Mrs. Nesbitt and I don't move. We exchange a look. I say, "He means, don't talk to Celeste."

"I feel married to her now," I tell Mrs. Nesbitt over supper. She smiles. "No wonder she wants me in Kansas

City—the store, money, belongings." We're quiet for a moment. "But there's more . . . that makes it harder."

"What?"

"Celeste is a hobo. She's desperate. She's counting on me. Part of me can't stand her, and the other part feels sorry for her."

Mrs. Nesbitt sighs. She's got the same intense expression she gets puzzling out one of her crosswords. "Kansas City is a lively place, Iris—lots of young people, opportunity, fun. Celeste would keep it . . . jazzy. Plus, Cecil and Dot don't live there, and it's not dusty like Wellsford. The schools are excellent."

I sink into my cellar inside. Why doesn't she just come out and say there's no room for me with Gladys Dilgert in Wellsford?

I hear the unexpected edge in my voice. "Mrs. Nesbitt, Celeste won't waste a minute luring another husband, and I'll be stuck with them forever at the Bootery." I picture myself sweeping foot powder off the floor, dizzy from staring at the crooked seams in our customers' stockings. "Plus, I already have enough credits to graduate from high school."

The kitchen swims. I can't swallow. "I'm sorry. I'm as mixed up as her." I look away, tears streaming down my cheeks. My mind escapes to Leroy wrapping himself so completely around me that I disappear.

Mrs. Nesbitt wipes her mouth, straightens her silverware. "Between the lines of that will I learned something about your father this afternoon that is quite remarkable."

"Yes?"

"You didn't trust him, with good reason . . . but his will, even the revised one, made one statement loud and clear: He trusted *you*."

CHAPTER 20

"So here are the slippers I talked to." I put them side by side on the rug Saturday morning.

Mrs. Nesbitt circles around as though analyzing a priceless sculpture. "How did they sound?"

"Ma'am? They didn't actually talk!"

"When he *walked*. Did they scuff, or drag, or flap?"

I think a moment, step in them and curl my toes. I circle the bedroom, trying different strides until I hit Daddy's rhythm—a crisp *creak, creak, creak*. "That's it," I say over my shoulder as I head out to the parlor. "He was a snappy stepper, always on the move, even at home.

"And this sound . . ." I close my eyes, shift my weight

on a squeaky floorboard by his desk. "I've heard it a thousand times. Then he'd sit and there'd be a long dramatic exhale—*unh*—at everything on his desk that he had to do. Next, he'd rub his sandpapery cheeks." I sit on his cane chair and find his fat, black fountain pen in the drawer. I stop. I'm little again, not allowed to touch it. "He sounded like a mouse—scritch-scratching his pen, rattling receipts, his cufflinks tapping on the blotter."

Mrs. Nesbitt sits on the divan with a satisfied smile. "Lovely! Dusting for sounds is so rewarding." She looks around. "Would you like to work with something else? Or is that enough?"

I sigh, staring blankly at Mama's piano, her secretary desk. I turn to Mrs. Nesbitt. "It's *enough* because dusting won't help me know what to *do* with all this hard old furniture, and Daddy's fancy pants and umbrella, and my dull bedspreads and broken dolls and third-grade schoolwork, and that stupid ugly clock. Oh, and then there's Celeste. There's absolutely not one thing to do with Celeste!"

I burst into tears. The next thing I know, I am walking into the kitchen to boil water. Mrs. Nesbitt and Henry follow.

On the summer's muggiest morning we sit drinking hot tea. I feel alert like Marie, waiting for something, absorbing every sound—the way the teaspoon clinks brightly on Mrs. Nesbitt's cup and dully on mine.

I look over at her. "Okay!" I say suddenly. "If you *insist*, I'll try Mama's brush."

She raises her eyebrows.

"I know exactly where it is." I head to my room and in a moment I am back, holding out Mama's old tortoiseshell hairbrush to Mrs. Nesbitt. "See . . . the handle isn't even rubbed down the way it's supposed to be in real life. She hardly got to use it."

Wound deep within the bristles I discover a single hair. I unwind it, lay it across my palm. It's long and dark and wavy. "I wonder if it's naturally curly or if it has just been in the brush so long."

Mrs. Nesbitt leans in, looks from my hand to my head. I pinch one end and lay Mama's hair on mine like a human halo.

She studies the situation, her glasses sparkling. "A perfect match!"

I go to the dining room to examine my head in the buffet mirror. Is the rest of me a perfect match for my mother?

"No doubt through the years your father made a strong, perhaps painful connection between you and your mother—your voices, expressions, mannerisms. Did he ever say so?"

"No." I look away, my insides uneasy. "He never spoke of it."

Once I've rewound the hair in the brush and wrapped it in a lace dresser scarf, Mrs. Nesbitt asks, "Would you consider cooking something?"

"What do you mean?"

"A recipe." Mrs. Nesbitt touches my elbow, guides me back to the kitchen.

"For what? The kitchen is already full of *condolence* food."

I carry the wooden recipe box to the table. "It's been mostly shut," I say, filing through. I stop at "Cottage Pudding" because the recipe card looks used—stained and bent. I hold it up. "Maybe Mama made this. Maybe she liked it."

"Let's decide she loved it," Mrs. Nesbitt says. "Is this her handwriting?"

"I'm not sure."

"It looks clear and unhurried. A bit rounded. Was your mother a bit *rounded*?"

"Not at the sanatorium. She was thin and hot with a wet washcloth on her forehead."

I grind the daylights out of our stiff old mixer. It clicks and bounces off the ceramic bowl. I crack eggs, scrape a wooden spoon. Mrs. Nesbitt asks, "Are any of these sounds familiar from before?"

"No."

I grease the glass cake pan, transfer the batter into it, and put it in the oven. We sit at the table, letting the scent of cottage pudding transform the room.

"You have no memories of being in here with her?" Mrs. Nesbitt asks.

"No, except that smell. The vanilla." I smile. "Or am I remembering your Anti-Pain Oil?"

After I wash the mixing bowls and spoons we eat the moist, steaming cake with applesauce on top.

"This is *internal* anti-pain medicine," Mrs. Nesbitt says, saluting heaven with her fork.

Later that afternoon Leroy and *I sit on our old picnic* table behind the church. I explain the pudding cake and all about dusting, even though I'm sure he's not the least bit interested. "It's not about dirt. It's finding what you thought you lost, making up what you never had." Leroy doesn't answer. "Sounds kinda strange, I guess." Leroy still doesn't reply. I look away. "So, anyway, I still have no idea what to *do* with everything." My cellar door opens. The ghosts are restless. "I can't stand to think about that."

"You can't take anything to Kansas City?"

"No. And I can't stand to think about that, either. I hate Kansas City."

I explain about Daddy's will. "So the only reason Celeste wants to be my guardian . . ."

Leroy turns to me, his eyes bright. "Is your money and the store." He counts on his fingers. "So let's see, you dread moving there. You don't trust her. You're not a shoe salesman. You'll end up living with some flashy new husband of hers someday. But you're just going to go right ahead and . . ."

I give him a *shut up* look. "In case you missed it, I don't have a choice for two whole years."

He's practically shouting. "God, Iris! What about the Nesbitts?"

I shout back. "Did you notice they haven't asked me? They can't, for some reason. Maybe it's Gladys Dilgert. Who knows why they don't want me there."

"Have you asked them?"

"NO!"

Leroy throws up his hands. "Oh, yeah, I forgot. Of course you don't *ask*, because you are a speck of dirt on God's Sunday-school shoes. You're just an orphan with fleas."

"Thank you so much. That was simply *beautiful*. You can really shut up now." I stare straight ahead at clumps of cattails sweeping the church steps. Top-heavy sunflowers droop, their leaves baked golden by the August sun.

Leroy reaches over, lifts my hair off my shoulder, tucks it behind my ear. I feel him looking at me. I stare at my lap. He touches the rim of my ear, outlines it. Then he traces around and around the inside curves with his fingertip.

"Ask me what I'm doing," he whispers.

My breath lifts and lowers me. "What are you doing, Leroy?"

"Dusting your ear."

Mrs. Nesbitt is on the porch swing. "I hear Marie, from a hundred miles away," she says as I come up the walk. "I sure miss her."

My heart is in my throat. I look her in the eye. "Mrs. Nesbitt?"

"Yes?"

The words pop right out. "I want you and Dr. Nesbitt to be my guardians."

I hear a sharp inhale. Mrs. Nesbitt stiffens and stares right past me over the chipped porch rail.

I take a breath. "And I do not want to live in Kansas City. I want to live in Wellsford with you."

Mrs. Nesbitt fumbles her hankie under her glasses. "Oh, these damn things."

I reach to help her, then pull back. "I'm sorry. I don't have . . . I'm . . ."

She motions for me to sit beside her, closes her eyes, gathers herself. She looks silvery and fragile. "Years ago, when my husband died, I thought I had suffered the big loss of my life." She works the damp hankie in her fingers. "I was sure I was protected from a repeat of that impossible pain. My turn was over."

The swing trembles. We stretch the beginnings of our spider's new home.

"But it wasn't." Her voice is soft and bitter. "In one irrational moment, in an unspeakable war"—she turns to me—"Morris was dead."

I barely breathe. I know she is working over a gash in her heart.

"We're the same, Iris. First your mother to tuberculosis, and then your father. Another senseless act—waging war with a train and the other ghosts he lived with." She shudders.

There's more in her, so I wait, just like she would.

"I'm old."

"Ma'am?"

"Kansas City is young and vibrant. So is Celeste. She'll be around a long while."

"You're old and vibrant."

She folds her gnarled hands and turns to me, a deep tenderness in her voice. "Lord knows Avery and I have discussed this, Iris. I've resisted because . . . don't you see? If you live with us you will lose me, too."

CHAPTER 21

Dear Celeste,

How are you? I am fine.
I am going to give the Bootery to you.
I sure hope you like it.

Dumb.

Dear Miss Celeste Simmons,

After consulting the attorney regarding my father's Last Will and Testament, I constitute, devise, and bequeath the Bootery to you.

You may also have any of his appurtenances and trappings, except his slippers. As the sole proprietor of the store, perhaps slippers would be a lofty accouterment to incorporate into your inventory.

Dumb, with spelling problems.

Dear Celeste,

I'm very sorry you are all alone and lonely, but remember, you are also young and vibrant. You will come out just fine even though I am not living with you.

Dear Celeste,

After searching my soul, I have decided to stay at the Nesbitts' and raise chickens. I hope you understand. . . .

I sit at Mama's little secretary desk. Balls of crumpled stationery dot the floor. It's hard to concentrate. Instead of clucks and the wind whining through the window casements, I hear the drips and murmurs of Atchison. A different house, a different song.

Henry taps up behind me.

"The most horrid letter is still better than the telephone or telling her to her face. The sooner she gets this, the better," I say, turning around to Mrs. Nesbitt. "I truly think she could do a good job with that store. Dr. Nesbitt thinks so too. She's got the personality. Daddy was really successful, and he had that same type of personality. I don't think she's going to mourn and moan for long, unless . . ." I lower my voice. "Unless she figures out a way to cash in on sympathy customers."

Mrs. Nesbitt sniffs.

"That was awful," I say. "I'm sorry. I . . ."

"I thought it the moment she climbed up the train steps with a twisted ankle. She's tougher than I'd first thought. Determined."

"It would be awful tripping around on a sprained ankle

pretending you are okay . . . always hurting and pretending you are okay."

"We all do it," Mrs. Nesbitt says.

August 25, 1926
Dear Celeste,

I have several things to say.

First, I am not moving to Kansas City. The Nesbitts have agreed to be my guardians and I am going to live with them in Wellsford.

Secondly, I have gone over my father's Last Will and Testament, and even though it was not signed, I want you to have the Bootery. Shoppers will like your handsome display windows and your enthusiasm.

The attorney will send you a letter about some money to help you get on your feet for the next six months. Carl, the manager of the Atchison store, has agreed to talk with you about business issues if you want his help.

I will rent out the house in Atchison

for now, until I decide if I am going to sell it. You can have any of Daddy's belongings you want, except his slippers and agate marbles and pen.
Best regards,
Iris

P.S. Mrs. Nesbitt says she thinks you will be a fine career woman, an example to modern young girls who wish to manage a business of their own. She says the Bootery will be the most successful retail establishment on Petticoat Lane!!!

There's only one shady spot in the letter: the part about Carl. But I know he'd help her if I asked him to. Carl has been great at managing Baldwin's Shoes since he came out of the back room. Proof, he says, that customers truly do trust somebody—even with stained fingernails—who knows shoes from the inside out.

Leroy leans on the back fender of Dr. Nesbitt's car. He has removed the legs from Mama's secretary desk and wedged it, wrapped in a quilt, onto the backseat, leaving a small spot for me to sit on the way back to Wellsford. We lashed the drawers and the sliding compartments shut. Mama's old papers and even a few books are still inside.

"So what's next?" he asks. He looks ready to lift the whole house with me in it.

"Let me think . . . dead weight being your specialty and all." He smiles, but I know down deep he hates for me to go. He called me a "complex animal" like it was a regal compliment. He also said that his mother said she remembered my mama was just beautiful.

I check my list, then point toward the house. "I need you to get the recipe card off the kitchen table, and Daddy's marbles and slippers."

We step onto the front porch. Leroy points up. "Did you want me to load that cobweb too?"

"Nope. The spider stays. But I do need you to get Mama's hair."

"Pardon me?"

"Unless it's too heavy. It's in my room wrapped in a dresser scarf."

I grip the side of Mama's secretary desk. Panic sprouts in me. "I need to go to the cemetery before we leave!"

Dr. Nesbitt slows the car, pulls to the shoulder.

"I'm sorry. I just . . . I can't . . ." The engine hums. The desk vibrates beside me. I search out the car window, my stomach full of crows. "Which direction is it? Where? It's . . . can anybody remember?"

Dr. and Mrs. Nesbitt exchange a look. He nods, cranks

the steering wheel, and heads south out of town. I tuck in corners of the desk quilt that have blown loose and stare through the front windshield.

They wait in the car while I run through the wrought iron gate to the mound of dirt over Daddy's grave—pebbles and clods covered with a pile of dead funeral flowers. There are ants and roly-poly bugs in it. So many busy creatures unearthed just to make room for him.

Mama's headstone is low and settled. It says: ANNA JANE KOHLER BALDWIN, 1885–1916.

I look from plot to plot. "It's me. I just wanted to say that I'm so sad to leave Atchison. But I have to." I glance back at the Ford waiting for me in the golden afternoon. "The house will be okay. I'm taking care of it." I turn to Daddy's side. "I gave Celeste the store, like you wanted. And Mama . . . we haven't spoken in a long time. Thank you for the desk. I have more of you yet to dust."

I look up at the clear sky and then at the headstones all around, mossy perches for ground squirrels and sparrows. I straddle the graves—a foot on each. I shift my weight side to side. The three of us together again.

My tears water the dirt. I'm not exactly like Mrs. Nesbitt, I think. Mama and Daddy and I didn't have the connection she describes with her husband and Morris, but . . . I am a moment they loved each other. I know that now.

I feel full and unexpectedly powerful. I wish I had something—not dead flowers and ribbons, but a real and lasting thing to leave for them. I step away, then turn back and take off my shoes. There is something permanent I can leave: my footprints—one in Daddy's dirt and the other a swirl in the fine dust over Mama.

The Nesbitts watch me walk to the car barefoot. "There's no hurry," Mrs. Nesbitt says out the window.

"I'm ready."

The sunflowers watch us turn around. Sun sparks off the weather-polished iron gate like a lightning strike. A choir of locusts tunes up.

We're all together too. Heading back north.

Homeward bound.

CHAPTER 22

"I remember something else Mama did."

Mrs. Nesbitt turns from the front seat of the car.

"She named me."

"Why of course. Is 'Iris' a family name?"

"No. Daddy wanted Louise, but she liked Iris." I turn my palms up. "And she won. So I'm Iris Louise Baldwin, not the other way around."

"So 'Iris' is a victory for your mother!" Mrs. Nesbitt looks genuinely pleased. "What does it mean?"

"I'll look it up right now." I read the slim *Naming Flowers* book I brought from our bookcase at home. *"'Iris, the Greek goddess of the rainbow, carries messages from the* gods and goddesses to favored mortals on Earth.' That's why I get along so well with my wallpaper! 'Widowers planted iris on the graves of their departed wives.'" I look up. "My father never did that."

"Which? Sorrowing or planting?" Dr. Nesbitt asks.

"Neither," I say flatly.

"My first name, Julia, means 'youthful,'" Mrs. Nesbitt says.

"That fits."

Dr. Nesbitt squares his shoulders and smiles at me in the rearview mirror. "Well, as one of you already knows, Avery means 'elf-ruler.'" He turns. "Doesn't it, Mother?"

Mrs. Nesbitt bows, turns to me. "I made that up when Avery and his brother were in their make-believe phase. Morris was hero of the heath!"

"Mother was cagey even then, Iris. Of course, being your guardian now, maybe elf-ruler fits!"

Mrs. Nesbitt unrolls her window and yells at the cows munching on what she calls Mother Earth's frayed summer dress: "I am Julia, ever-youthful, Elizabeth Thornhill Nesbitt."

Dr. Nesbitt honks. "Avery, elf-ruler. Thomas Nesbitt." He honks again.

The car rattles down the road. I inform the wind and gnats and hay, "I am Iris Louise, not-the-other-way-around. Baldwin. Iris Louise Baldwin."

Dr. Nesbitt honks two long honks and finally the cows turn, nameless spectators at Mama's rowdy one-car victory parade.

Dot rolls her cold little eyes. "Oh, good, you're back."
She has a fistful of clothespins.

"So your Pa's dead." She lolls her head. "I guess you're
the only Baldwin still left to croak." She looks heavenward. "Oh, I forgot, you ain't gonna croak 'cause you're
still a baby." Dot sucks her thumb. "Please, Dr. Nesbitt, Grandmommy Nesbitt, I'm Iris the helpless infant.
Please take me in." She slurps and wags her hips.

In less than two weeks time she's worse. A chill runs
through me imagining that innocent baby. It should
be scared to be born, the way I am scared of the horrid
thought that has been born in me and won't go away. . . .

I march in the house, straight into my room, slam the
door, and pace. The wallpaper goddesses float around
me in their mythological world, a place where everything
shocking—murder, lying, jealousy, adultery, double-
crossing, incest—has happened.

"There's a Greek tragedy happening right here in
Wellsford, Missouri. At the farm next door," I whisper
to the muses. "The girl there is pregnant . . . but nobody
can talk about it. Her father hurts her, I've seen the
marks, and . . . ," I cover my mouth, barely uttering the
idea that has begun to haunt me. "I think he might . . .
be . . . the . . . baby's . . . father."

I turn to the buffet mirror, shocked to see my face looking fierce, older. "There. You finally said it."

I walk out, pull the door shut, leaving my despicable
secret thought with the goddesses.

"Cecil and Dot are like having a volcano in the backyard," Mrs. Nesbitt says at supper. She glances in the direction of their farmhouse. "They're going to erupt. When do you think the baby is due, Avery?"

"Three months, maybe four." Dr. Nesbitt wipes his mouth. "Cecil was here twice while you two were in Atchison. His stomach, his rump. His face was as fiery as a hill of red ants."

Mrs. Nesbitt puts down her fork. "Oh, thank you, as always, for the grisly details of Cecil's medical woes."

"I offered to give Dot a checkup, since she'd been feeling sick for quite a while, but Cecil wouldn't hear of it. He said she was just a complainer." Dr. Nesbitt's face is grim. "There is no winner in this mess. A wild river of urges and moonshine flows through that man."

I take a deep breath, force the words. "If you'll forgive me for saying something terrible, Cecil acts different with me when one of you isn't around. I think with enough moonshine Cecil might act out his—urges—on anybody, *any* . . . girl." I wipe my eyes.

Mrs. Nesbitt gives me a penetrating look. "You mean *Dot*, don't you?"

"Maybe . . ."

Dr. Nesbitt works his jaw.

"Do you think he might have *touched* Dot?" Mrs. Nesbitt says evenly. "More than just bruises?"

I nod.

"It's a rusty old world," Dr. Nesbitt says with uncharacteristic bitterness. He sighs. "We can't address that. We'll never know. But we sure do know the Deetses can turn on anyone, like Iris just said—even each other."

I clasp my hands on the table, lean in. "But with that baby, Dot needs someplace away from him."

We sit silent.

"Nothing good is in store for that child, no matter who the father is—problems all the elf-leaders on Earth can't fix." Mrs. Nesbitt puts her hand on mine, smiles wearily. "Are you sure you don't want to change your mind about living in Kansas City?"

"Let's all go," Dr. Nesbitt says, gazing out the window.

"I hope you'll put this in the front room," Mrs. Nesbitt says. We stand by Mama's secretary, still parked in the entry hall.

"Mrs. Nesbitt? That's Morris's room."

She waves her hands. "Oh, I'm changing that. It was a well-appointed tomb, not a living room." She smiles. "I told Morris, and he seemed relieved! You can fill it as you please, just so long as we can fit in there too. Lord knows we need the space now." She taps down the hall and into the parlor followed by Marie, who sniffs every nook and cranny like a dealer in rare antiques.

In minutes Dr. Nesbitt and I have moved the desk and chair, and taken the cloth off the mysterious oil painting over the piano. I study the picture.

"It's me." Mrs. Nesbitt sighs, points with her cane. "Avery's dear friend Marsden painted it after Morris died."

It's an angled back-view of a woman seated at a piano. Her hands are folded on the keys, her spine curved, her head bent. Her brilliant gold and red shawl contrasts with her deeply shadowed face. She is not looking at the music. It's impossible to tell if she's afraid to go ahead and touch the piano keys, if she's exhausted from playing, or if she's praying for inspiration. The streaks and dabs of color are so vivid, you can imagine the artist's hands flying.

But the mood is sad.

"I—she—was stuck," Mrs. Nesbitt says matter-of-factly. "Marsden did a perfect rendering of me at that time, but it was too true. That's why I covered it up. But now"—she sweeps her hand—"she'll have the company of our new family members, Anna Jane Baldwin and her daughter."

We spend the afternoon rearranging, scrubbing, polishing, and sorting the parlor. "These figurines don't look as hostile as they used to," Dr. Nesbitt says. "And the love seat feels less like a horse with rigor mortis."

"I guess the whole room was grumpy that I left it for dead."

I am minding my own business in the chicken house when Pansy Deets pops in my mind as surely as if she had walked up and tapped me on the forehead. "Go away, Pansy," I say out loud. "A lot of help you are these days."

But in the parlor I find myself flipping through Mama's *Naming Flowers* book. *Pansy: from the French* penser, *meaning* "*to think*." Well, that doesn't fit. I would hardly call her thoughtful. I close the book, fighting the impossible idea forming in my mind.

I tell Marie, who sits with me on my bed, "Pansy is long gone. She vanished in the night, hightailed it on Mrs. Nesbitt's generosity. There is no way she'll ever show up again." I scratch Marie's ears. "On the other hand . . . if Pansy could make herself disappear, why couldn't she help Dot vanish too?" I shake my head, hoping this idea will fall right out on the floor where it belongs. I can't bring it up because Mrs. Nesbitt has sworn off meddling with that woman. Who can blame her?

I picture Pansy: a straggly, beaten down woman, unsmart, unloved, but hopefully unbruised—at least for now. I picture Cecil: his grubby hands on her neck, his expression always mocking the heart of everything and everyone. "Everybody despises Cecil as much as you do, Marie. He's not fit to be a log on the Devil's woodpile."

I imagine what Dot has seen and heard and felt, being raised by him. How could she ever risk telling him no about anything? How will her baby have a prayer of growing up all right? I feel sick inside. Compared to hers and her baby's, my life is a piece of angel food cake.

"Mrs. Nesbitt?" I say the moment she awakens from her nap. "I've been thinking . . ."

"If it's what I'm thinking . . ." Her eyes fill with pain. "I'm warning both of us: we cannot and will not take Dot in."

"Yes, ma'am. I know."

"And Avery cannot be her doctor. We cannot give her money to run away. We cannot prove anything."

"I know." My stomach flutters. I force the words. "Dot needs her mama."

Tears come to Mrs. Nesbitt's eyes. She sniffs, looks at me, bewildered. Without meaning to I have stirred up her worst feelings of regret and responsibility.

CHAPTER 23

"Tongue depressors, quilting scraps, apple butter, Bee Secret, Digestive Support Powder, thread, Avery, cottage pudding." I check the supplies while Mrs. Nesbitt calls out our list.

"Avery won't stay in the box," I say.

"Well, who needs him anyway?"

We're heading to Ruthie's house. I hope it will lift our spirits. Mrs. Nesbitt hasn't mentioned Dot since my extraordinarily poor idea about Pansy. I feel so bad about it, my constant sighing has created a cloud over everybody's head.

Ruthie's cat greets us, leaving a trail of muddy paw prints

across the hood of the car. Cora, standing on the lopsided porch, looks somewhere between dead and elated. Ruthie is nowhere in sight.

Mrs. Nesbitt supervises the unloading of our boxes and bags and gives Cora the Rawleigh salves and powder. I notice cozy beds created from two dresser drawers. But for now the twins lie side by side on the bed. They are a miracle to look at, and we just stare, lapping up their sweet squirminess.

Dr. Nesbitt warms the stethoscope on his palm before he examines their perfect little cantaloupe-shaped chests. They follow his wiggling fingers with luminous blue-gray eyes.

Silent as a spider, Ruthie weaves her hand in mine. She's fresh-faced and happy to see me, a far cry from the frightened girl blinking at my flashlight a month ago. We make dolls by wrapping tongue depressors together with yarn and dressing them. At Ruthie's request we make Little Bo Peep, an elephant with two legs and two trunks, a queen, and a mouse in a top hat.

Mrs. Nesbitt sits regally with a twin lined up on each arm. Dr. Nesbitt examines Cora, then fixes her a fat square of cottage pudding. "Nursing these handsome fellas, you need to eat three times as much as that husband of yours." Dr. Nesbitt winks at Ellis and cuts him a piece too.

We don't do much of anything, really, just feel the easy pace of rocking and humming and patting, discussing if the twins are identical and saying kind and hopeful things. Dr. Nesbitt is the master of that. His tenderness, even with Ellis, and his free-flowing advice are better than a whole Rawleigh wagon full of elixirs.

I wonder why he's never married, had children of his own.

"Olive Nish knew her and her sister," Mrs. Nesbitt mutters. She looks up, as though surprised to hear her own voice.

"Is that a clue for your crossword puzzle?" I ask.

She sighs, pats her hair. "If only it were that simple."

Dr. Nesbitt steps into the kitchen from his office. The patient he's been seeing and her mother drive off. He has just removed a hornet stinger out of the little girl's arm using a butter knife. "The best piece of medical equipment I have," he says, wiping it with alcohol. "The right angle, a slight pressure, and pop, it's out!"

I smile and turn to Mrs. Nesbitt, who seems to have forgotten about her puzzle. I go back to mending a pair of threadbare yard pants.

Mrs. Nesbitt mutters, "But Olive is such a snoop. . . ."

"How many letters is your word?" I ask. "Could it be . . . 'eavesdropper'?"

"No, Iris, I'm not *doing* the puzzle."

"Ma'am?"

She turns to her son. "Isn't it true, Avery, that if I picked up the phone right this minute and somebody was conversing on the party line, I could just say 'Olive, are you listening in?' And before she could stop herself, she'd answer, 'Why yes, of course I am.'"

"That woman knows more about the medical condition of Wellsford than I do." He studies his mother, then turns to me, puzzled. "Why are we discussing Olive Nish and her formidable meddling expertise? Have you been eavesdropping on *her*?"

"No, sir. I've never heard of her until just now."

Mrs. Nesbitt straightens her shoulders. "Iris had a provocative notion the other day, the bud of a plausible solution for Dot's predicament."

Dr. Nesbitt sits down, shakes his head. "Oh, boy. A provocative notion, a plausible solution. Some scheme involving Olive Nish? Look no further folks, the volcano's gonna blow. You know if you try to help, Dot could use you just like Pansy did."

"Of course I know that, Avery. Do you think I'm nuts?"

"Yes. So how could Olive help Dorothy Deets?" he asks.

Marie perks her ears. Mrs. Nesbitt raises her eyebrows, looks at me, then at her son.

"Olive could help find Dot's mother. She's the only person I know who had Pansy's acquaintance besides me. And she knows Pansy's sister."

"Pansy? The '*passed-on*' Pansy?" Dr. Nesbitt slumps his shoulders. "Oh, God, raising the dead."

"She's not dead."

"She's gonna wish she was."

He turns to me for an explanation.

"I . . . I . . . well, I thought since Pansy had slipped away a while ago now, maybe she was sorry for it, and if she knew Dot was in trouble she might come back and do what she should have done in the first place: take Dot with her."

Dr. Nesbitt stands up. "So if you locate Pansy, are you three going to tell her that Dot's expecting? What if Olive rats on you to Cecil, or the whole town for that matter?" He taps the side of his head. "Olive isn't as sharp as she once was, she could spill the beans to the wrong party without meaning to."

We look up at him. There are tears in Mrs. Nesbitt's eyes. He sits again. We all sink into silence.

"I caused this," Mrs. Nesbitt says, her voice softened with guilt. "The baby has no hope living with Cecil. He will treat it as cursed, no matter who the father is, no matter what kind of problems it has."

Dr. Nesbitt takes his mother's hand, his expression troubled and tired. He turns to me. "Talk it over with the goddesses, Iris. We mortals need divine guidance."

I slip on my nightgown, toss my hairclip on the bed, and shake my head. The house is quiet except for the wind and Marie, who moans and twitches in her dreams beside me. She must still have the screeching rhythm of the train buried deep inside from her hobo-living days.

I light a candle on my little dresser and kneel on the rug in front of it. I address the wallpaper. "Okay, goddesses, we need to talk some more." My voice sounds rich and solemn. The flame dances. The walls seem to lean in. "You know about the tragedy. Everybody involved is awful, except for this little baby."

I feel their ancient eyes on me.

"You all have been through this kind of thing before, and so . . ."

Get the flower book, they say.

I retrieve the book from Mama's desk in the parlor, kneel again, and read to myself: *Pansy: from the viola family, familiar to people living in fifth-century B.C. Greece.* I salute the goddesses and continue. *Resembles a human face. Cold-hardy, will survive a freeze even during the blooming period.*

Well, it's boiling-hot August here, but the hearts involved are frozen, so maybe she's hardy enough to show her face to Dot.

Anything else? I silently ask the goddesses.

Remember, Iris, you are smarter than Cecil Deets.

I stare at the thin pillar of candle smoke rising, floating out to the goddesses. I let my eyes go blurry so the flame fills my head. "Marie," I whisper, "that last part sounded more like Leroy talking." I hug myself. I wonder what he's doing right now. I look out at the endless night. Is he staring at the star-gods over Atchison, thinking about me? A shimmery feeling floods through me. I take a long, deep breath and hold it.

I am the Goddess Iris, powerful enough to turn Leroy into the warm, wet air captured inside me.

CHAPTER 24

"*Your first impression of Olive Nish is paramount,*" Mrs. Nesbitt says as I press the brake by her ramshackle house on the edge of Wellsford. The yard backs up to the bluff of a dry riverbed. "We must be positive Olive will help us. We can't have her blabbering to Cecil how we plan to resurrect Pansy and have her kidnap his own blood child."

Between two front-door stoops sits a dusty garden with rusted zinnias and heat-choked pansies. Mrs. Nesbitt clears her throat. We exchange a wary glance.

"Can't we just inquire about Pansy without giving the reason?" I whisper fast as Mrs. Nesbitt rings the doorbell.

"She'll know we have a reason."

I shake my head. "We can't say there's a desperate matter requiring Pansy's attention without . . ." The door opens.

Olive Nish makes Mrs. Nesbitt look like the strong woman in a circus. A huge rhinestone clip tugs at the neck of her purple housedress. Her face is tiny, with a beaky nose and papery cheeks that could use some sunshine. She carries a black patent-leather pocketbook.

"Oh, excuse us, Olive, were you on your way out?"

"No. Come in and sit." We face her on stiff dining-room chairs. Her dingy house smells of sour milk and mothballs. She looks me over. "This must be Iris. Condolences about your father and the turmoil with his fiancée—Celeste Simmons, isn't it? You certainly have had your hands full taming that gal." She shakes her head. "And with your own grief to bear."

So Olive knows all. I glance at her phone, imagine the receiver still warm from her last eavesdropping session.

She asks after Dr. Nesbitt, the "medical genius" of all Missouri. We exchange other pleasantries. Without warning, and without checking my supposed intuitive gift, I leap right off the forbidden cliff. "Miss Nish, might you know how we could contact Pansy Deets?"

Olive digs through the pocketbook tucked in next to her. She pops a lozenge in her mouth, sucks it noisily. The telephone rings, but she stays put.

"There's a bit of a desperate matter, Olive . . ." Mrs. Nesbitt says, leaping right along with me.

Olive cocks her head, points to the wall. "Hear that?" Her eyes narrow. "My renters have a dog." She shakes a finger. "They *know* I strictly forbid canines on my property." She turns to me, looking all the world like a chicken. "That dog wee-wees on my foundation a hundred times a day. Drop by drop he's soaking it to ruins."

I picture Miss Nish seated on her needlepoint settee crashing through to the cellar.

"A canine, ma'am?"

Miss Nish studies us. I can almost see the dog trot right out of her mind. "Pansy's daughter, Dorothy, is expecting," she states, snapping shut both her mouth and her pocketbook. "She walked past here yesterday and the day before. I saw it clear as day."

We stare at each other, stone-faced.

Miss Nish's expression turns dark. "Dorothy needs her mother now. Isn't that why you're here? *Mister* Deets is a controversial figure, to say the least. After how he treated poor Pansy . . ."

"How did you know about Dot?"

"It doesn't require reading apple seeds, no crystal ball needed to interpret a pregnant belly."

"So you . . . ?"

She thinks a moment. "I can attempt a correspondence with Pansy's sister in Chicago; she might know her whereabouts. But we three need to stick together . . . never, ever, even on our deathbeds—swear on a Bible or burn in Hell—will you tell Cecil I had one peep of involvement."

Mrs. Nesbitt nods.

I clear my throat, straighten my back. "We further understand why *you* can never—cross your heart, shake of salt, thump a banana—*ever* tell Cecil Deets that Mrs. Nesbitt and I had one peep of involvement either."

"Agreed," she says with a snap of her fingers.

"Agreed." I snap back. "We are going to need some of Pansy's belongings too—preferably something old that Dot would recognize."

Mrs. Nesbitt turns to me, bewildered.

"And," I continue, "we cannot communicate by telephone for obvious reasons."

Olive's eyes flash. "Dorothy Deets and I already have a silent telephone connection."

"Really?"

She leans in. "The girl calls, then doesn't talk. It's happened several times lately. I know the cadence of her breathing."

"Why would she?"

"She's aware I knew her Mama," Miss Nish whispers. "It's a cry for help."

"*Do you really think Dot phones her?*" I ask as we get in the car.

Mrs. Nesbitt rolls her eyes. "I couldn't predict Dot, but Olive hears lots of things that aren't there. Have you ever known someone to carry a pocketbook around their own home?"

"Do you think her renters have a dog?" I ask, gazing at the crumbling stoop.

"I don't think she has renters!"

I smile. "Well, this will give her something real to deal with."

I drive away, imagining Cecil—that lump of evilness—passed out on the floor and Dot, clutching her baby belly, silently panting in the telephone: *Somebody help!*

*I will spend this afternoon going over Mama's secre-*tary desk and the things in it, one at a time. I will understand them just the way Mrs. Nesbitt would, as bits of the person Mama was, and maybe who I am too. But I feel afraid to touch the traces of the old me I'll find inside.

I'm alone except for the beautiful, poignant portrait of Mrs. Nesbitt watching me from above the piano. I understand how she, too, hesitated at the task ahead of her—grieving for her husband and Morris.

The front-room windows gleam after our cleaning session. The secretary and matching chair fit nicely along the piano wall. The desk is worn mahogany with a long middle drawer under the writing top. Above are stacks of cigar box–sized drawers, cubbyholes, and two long compartments with sliding tops.

Divots and dashes, bits of old words and salutations, are etched into the varnish on the writing surface—the tracks of Mama's fountain pen. I close my eyes and slide my fingers back and forth, but the marks are too delicate to feel. I trace them with her dry pen, study my hand moving the way hers did. I wonder if her fingernails curved like mine. Did she wear more than a wedding band? Did she sit here knowing her life would be cut short?

I stop my hand, but I can't stop my tears.

That was morbid.

No more morbid.

The secretary moans like it's stiff and sore when I open the drawer where Mrs. Andrews let me keep my old Cray-olas. I remember wondering when I was little why all eight colors smelled alike—how could yellow possibly be the same as black? The paper is peeled completely off of the violet and blue ones. They are only stubs from all the skies full of robins and angels I have colored.

Folded with a paper clip in the main drawer are the six pictures I drew then of Mama—a happy angel floating above the sanatorium, wearing each of her pairs of shoes. Across the front porch of the hospital are flowers and rocking chairs full of patients. It looks like a gay garden party.

Hi, Mama.

I turn over one drawing, take a pencil, and before I know it, I start a picture of this desk. It begins okay, but I get bogged down doing the complicated angles and corners. My shading on the cubby holes is wrong and the legs look crippled.

Damn.

I try a rubbing of the marks in the desktop, the way people do on old-time gravestones. But none of Mama's handwriting comes through.

In my mind I see that same mocking expression of Daddy's, hear him scoff, *Well, Iris, looks like your drawing skills didn't move with you to Wellsford. . . .*

Shut up, ghosts.

I remember being so sure back then that Mama was still real after she died, that she had just moved to the sky. It made as much sense as anything. But really she just floated away from me. Not like a kite that tugs mightily and breaks its string, but slowly—day by day, a little at a time, as she got sicker.

I look again at my picture, how I've colored Daddy and me in our wagon heading home. I always did it that way, with us leaving.

A thought about her slips into my mind from a new angle, sheds stark light on the picture. How must it have been for her to watch me leave Sunday after Sunday? There was so little we could say or do during the visits, especially with the storm cloud of Daddy there, so impatient to go the second anything got sad. He just would not have it.

She couldn't tuck me in, brush my hair, dust me . . .

Instead of a healthy, loved angel, I see her in a lonely waiting room for mothers who have lost their little girls.

I bow my head and sit there for a long while. I still have the side compartments to go through. But not today. In the back of one upper cubbyhole I spot something: a clear paperweight with colored glass flowers inside. Although they are too small, I decide they are irises. The globe feels solid and whole. I warm it in my hands, turn it over. An *X* and an *O* are scratched in the bottom.

I close my eyes and rub my fingers over the etched hug and kiss. Who gave this to her? Daddy?

What does it matter?

Mama just gave it to me.

CHAPTER 25

It's been two weeks with no smoke signal from Olive.

I feel like a walking fishbowl with the Pansy plot circling inside—will Olive find her? Will Pansy cooperate? Will Dot? And Cecil . . . oh God, *Cecil!*

A thousand times a day I think, *C'mon Dot, give us another sign. The goddesses are rooting for you. Call Olive and breathe for help.*

But so far, the only change in Dot is that she has stopped calling me a baby and has started calling me a bitch. The double-barrel of her mouth is even more lethal since the Nesbitts cancelled Gladys Dilgert. I'm not plain-old-orphan hired help, a fish without a bowl. I belong here.

I know it has started a stew of pure jealousy cooking in Dot.

Lots of people would say, *Just let those creepy Deets have each other.* But the baby stirs something in all of us. And hopefully, maybe, there is the thin shred of a chance it is stirring something in Dot.

While reading his newspaper after dinner, Dr. Nesbitt remarks, "You and mother don't exactly have poker faces . . . or mouths, for that matter. Cecil's wily. He'll sniff something brewing, especially if it's moonshine—or involves Pansy."

Mrs. Nesbitt gives him an exaggerated blank expression. "We know that, Avery. That's why we've both vowed to avoid him—not that it's any sacrifice. Couldn't you give Cecil some knockout pills until Dot's long gone?"

"Knockout pills?"

"Well, I don't know . . . something." She slumps, sighs.

"Actually," Dr. Nesbitt says, "this plan of yours is so full of holes, it just might work."

"Speaking of holes . . . ," Mrs. Nesbitt says slowly, turning to me. "I've been meaning to ask you, Iris. Do you know how to shoot?"

"Ma'am?"

"A gun."

"No."

Dr. Nesbitt lowers the paper. "Why don't you show her, Mother?"

"Any bona fide farm woman should know," Mrs. Nesbitt says. "Don't you agree, Avery?"

"Absolutely. Without the threat of a farm woman with gun skills, a fox could tip his hat to Marie, waltz right into the coop, and exit chewing a chicken leg." Dr. Nesbitt puts down his paper, picks up the shotgun, and aims it out the back door. He glances skyward. "We've still got a few hours of light. Would you please hang our target, Iris, while I back the car into the next county?"

I pin an old sheet to the clothesline and shut Marie in the house.

Mrs. Nesbitt is very particular about my technique. She demonstrates proper form by planting her feet just so, raising Henry to her shoulder, and squinting down the barrel of him.

Dr. Nesbitt hops out of range. "Is Henry loaded?"

"This is called a 'side by side.' Two barrels." He inserts a cartridge in each side, cocks the hammers, and shoots the sheet. Once. Twice. We walk into the yard to study the shot pattern. "We already know you've got crackerjack aim with an egg, Iris." He points to the piercings in the cotton. "If your coyote is unusually tall, say he's up on his hind legs and he's got a flaming rear end, you can scare him by aiming high."

"Does the predator in question answer to the name Deets?" Mrs. Nesbitt asks, her face wary. "If he knows we helped steal a chicken from his house, don't we also know he'll try to steal one from ours?"

I practice shooting a dozen times—at the sheet, the broad side of the shed, and at cans on a sawhorse.

"It's easier than cooking, but I'm still terrible," I say,

dizzy and sore from the kickbacks, the gun powder, and the ringing in my ears. "I suppose if a real coyote came, I'd have to ask him to pose in front of the sheet for me to kill him. Besides, I can't hurt anybody. Any self-respecting target will know that. They'll think I look like a fool."

"You may surprise yourself." Dr. Nesbitt turns to his mother. "Right?"

Mrs. Nesbitt nods. "Remember to aim high. You just want to threaten, to scare. That's all."

Dr. Nesbitt levels me with a grave look. "And Iris, you are anything but a fool."

I weigh the envelope from Leroy on my hand as I walk up from the mailbox. Two pages? Three? I position it, still sealed, next to me on the elm tree bench and imagine what's inside.

I hope he's saying he'll be here in a month for my birthday.

I swat a grasshopper off my skirt and look around. Sigh. It's already turning into fall. I imagine the Missouri River bluffs in Atchison painted with red vine. I smell burning leaves and hear my neighbors complain that oaks keep their dull brown foliage clear till Thanksgiving. I picture my old school. I'm through with that now—although Mrs. Nesbitt insists we still have much to discuss on the education topic.

Inside the envelope are two heavy sheets of paper, but not a single word.

Drawn on one is an outline of Leroy's left hand and on the other is his right. I smooth out the folds and arrange them on my lap with thumbs pointing at each other. His fingers are long, the contours strong, almost elegant. No one else has hands like Leroy's.

Stars—constellations—are drawn around the outlines in midnight-blue ink. I picture him studying his star chart, drawing them, careful not to smear.

I place my palms on his. Stretch my fingers and take a deep breath.

Hi, Leroy.

Still anchored to the paper, I look into the afternoon sky. The moon is a bleached opal. The brassy sun outshines the Big Dipper.

I hold the papers against both cheeks. I close my eyes and imagine night blooming all around the two of us. I slide his hands over my lips and down my neck.

Something flutters by. Oh, God! My eyes snap open. I scan the yard. It's just a curious little dirt-brown bird. "Oh! I just . . . it's a letter . . . I . . ."

It blinks at me and hops away.

I put the papers on my lap. "I miss you, Leroy."

I hear him whisper: *Send something to me.*

I know immediately what I want to send back.

"It's Olive Nish for you, Avery," Mrs. Nesbitt yells through his office door late Thursday evening.

We can hear Olive's voice through the line as Dr.

Nesbitt listens and nods. She seems to have a vague but mighty pain in her left lower quadrant that takes her "breath away."

My heart sinks. Olive's sick.

"Make a house call," Mrs. Nesbitt whispers to her son. "We need Olive at full steam. There's nothing of her to wither. We need her probing for Pansy, not suffering with a queasy quadrant."

Mrs. Nesbitt and I drink tea to pass the time. I read aloud an article from an old *Atlantic Monthly* magazine of Dr. Nesbitt's entitled "Art and the X-ray."

Mrs. Nesbitt recalls some of the gustatory medical "payments" her son has received from Olive over the years. "Each one etches its own signature on the stomach."

"So he helps her feel better, and she makes you two sick!"

"Exactly. It's the unlikely mix of ingredients in her food, the texture . . . the odd bitter twist to her tomato aspic, her gravelly gravy, her pulpy sweet potatoes . . ." She shudders. Shuts her mouth.

Moths bounce off the table lamp. Marie yawns for the hundredth time. Olive's malady must be serious, judging from the clock.

Finally Dr. Nesbitt's headlights wind up the drive. He walks in with a towel-covered metal baking pan large enough to hold hay for a herd of buffalo.

We hop to our feet. "Well . . . ? What's wrong? What's Olive got?"

Dr. Nesbitt's face is dead serious. He whispers, "Pansy."

Mrs. Nesbitt holds her throat.

My heart flutters. "On the phone?" I ask, as stupid as can be.

"No. She's at Olive's house."

"Right now?"

"Yep. Pansy at this moment is lodging with Olive's invisible renters and their equally invisible dog."

"Did you see her? Talk?"

"Yes."

"Are you sure? I mean . . . of course, but what . . . what have you got there?" Mrs. Nesbitt eyes the casserole.

"Proof."

He puts the pan on the table and lifts the towel. On top is a ratty nightgown and under it a brown knit shawl. "All Pansy's stuff, just what you asked for, Iris," he says with a flourish. He lifts out a knotted hankie. Taps it on his palm. "Full of silver dollars."

"Why did she give you silver dollars?" Mrs. Nesbitt asks.

"Olive thought you'd figure a use for them. Dot's a crow when it comes to something shiny."

Mrs. Nesbitt pats her stomach. "So Pansy knows about Dot and all?"

"I believe Olive has been quite blunt with Pansy regarding Dot."

"How'd Pansy get here?"

Dr. Nesbitt shakes his head. "Olive's lips are sealed." He does a pinched-voiced, bent-over Olive imitation. "I'll carry the burden. No one need know the details but me. I love intrigue of this persuasion."

Mrs. Nesbitt and I exchange a look. We asked for Pansy,

we got Pansy. There's no turning back. We are meddlers, to be sure, but only apprentices compared to Madam Nish.

"Your job, according to Olive, is to lure Dot to the Nish residence," Dr. Nesbitt says. "And Olive's magic trick is to make Dot and Pansy disappear."

CHAPTER 26

The ace poker players have stacked the deck—actually the laundry basket. We're about to "play cards" with Dot.

The basket—or as Dr. Nesbitt calls it, "the bait"—is on the back porch waiting for her arrival.

Marie plays possum beside it. Dr. Nesbitt is at work and Mrs. Nesbitt and I are positioned behind the blinds in her bedroom. I'm on my knees and Mrs. Nesbitt sits in her old wheelchair rolled to the window. I have just cleaned her glasses so we both have a perfect view of the washing machine. My stomach is a double knot. Mrs. Nesbitt swears she swallowed her tea bag at breakfast.

Dot plods up the driveway in a flimsy checked dress,

mopping her forehead on this Indian summer morning. Her expression is sour as usual. She does not have one clue that she is about to make the biggest choice of her life. She can free herself from Cecil's grip, take her fate and her baby's future into her very own hands.

But will she?

Dot peers through the back door with a "where is everybody" look. She scowls, no doubt disappointed I am not handy to spit on. She stretches her back. Scratches her big belly.

Inside we strain at the window to detect one tiny bit of softness in her touch, a gentle pat, a reflective sigh.

Nothing.

Dot yanks one, two, three towels off the pile in the basket. She inspects and sniffs each one and stuffs them in the tub. I know she's figuring out which towel each of us used during the week.

Mrs. Nesbitt takes my hand as we watch Dot peer deep in the basket. Her eyes shift. She stops, scratches her behind, looks again. She slowly pulls out her mother's dingy lavender-gray nightgown, the way someone would remove a person's bloody bandage.

She shakes it out and just stares and stares. I swear I see Marie open one snake eye. Dot crushes the gown in her fists, then raises it to her nose.

C'mon, Dot. Keep going. We shift to try and see her expression, but all we get is that pug profile.

Dot claws through the next level of clothes. Stops short at Pansy's shawl.

Mrs. Nesbitt holds her hands in prayer point. "Put it on, Dot. Wrap up in it."

Instead Dot drops it on the floor and bangs a fist on our back door.

We stay silent and absolutely motionless.

She bangs again. "Shit!"

Dot turns and marches off the porch. Her face is fiery, like her father's. She scans the yard, yanks open the shed, then the coop. She struts and stirs the chicken yard into a meringue of feathers.

She's after me. Next she'll stomp right in the house, waving the gown and screaming, "What're you doing, you bitch?"

Instead Dot plops down on the porch step, her back to us. We want desperately for her to sob. We want her to smell her mama in the shawl, stroke her own cheek with it. "Dust the shawl," Mrs. Nesbitt and I coach softly. We ache for her to put two and two together, to realize this answers her cry for help.

More than anything we want her to not run home.

Marie rouses, pads across the porch, and places her paws on the laundry basket. She whines as though it's her empty supper bowl. Dot stands, turns, still holding her mother's clothes, and shoos Marie off. She eyes the basket with a suspicious sneer that is pure Cecil.

"Okay, Dorothy, find the money," Mrs. Nesbitt barely whispers from the bedroom.

Dot claws down through the basket, her eyes darting this way and that. I think she senses it's a trap, and she's right. She's used to being hunted.

Find the money.

Find the money.

Dot lifts the hankie full of silver dollars and pulls open the knot. She sits cross-legged on the floor and lines up the coins, which we have polished to an irresistible shine, across her lap.

She examines each coin, even tries to bite one. Dot unfolds the little paper we put inside that reads: *For more $ go to Olive's.*

The dollar sign jolts Dot like smelling salts. She hurriedly pockets the silver, then wraps the nightgown and shawl into one of our towels and ties it. She looks this way and that, clutching her Mama's belongings, and hurries down the driveway.

Don't go left. Don't go home. Go right. Go to Olive's. Please . . . turn right to Olive's.

Mrs. Nesbitt elbows me. Smiles. Dot has stopped long enough to wad the note, pop it in her mouth, and swallow it.

Brilliant!

Dot takes off running toward Olive's without so much as a backward glance, her heavy pocket clanking against her stomach.

I let out the breath I have been holding for at least an hour. Mrs. Nesbitt shakes her head and says, "Pansy knows her girl. Money talks."

"Where do you think the two, uh, three of them will go?"

"Anywhere without a forwarding address. That excludes

Pansy's sister, and they obviously can't stay at Olive's. What we don't know can only *help* us. Especially if we get the third degree from You Know Who."

"All we did was fill the laundry basket, same as every other Monday," I say. "But what'll Dot and Pansy use for money? Ten dollars isn't enough for expenses and train fare for two."

Mrs. Nesbitt raises her eyebrows. "I have an inkling Olive's pocketbook is deeper than it looks. That's probably the reason she never lets it go!"

All day we imagine Dot and Pansy on the train, on the road, on the run—two hobos with the sheer force and funding of Olive Nish behind them.

Despite my permanent case of nerves, and the fear that Cecil's going to spring out of the closet at me, there is also a new and true feeling.

I am a part of something important.

"Haven't you noticed," I say to Marie later in my room, "that when you truly belong somewhere, there's more to do?"

She nudges me with her nose.

I scratch her back. "I wish I had known *your* mother. She must have been quite a gal to have a daughter like you!"

"The stamp is upside down. Better not open it." The postman winks when he hands me the mail. "Bad omen."

Of course I can already see that. It's a letter from Celeste.

September 9, 1926
Dear Iris,

I have no one to tell but you.

I'm blue.

I try every which way to cover it up, to not smear my face. I keep my stiff upper lip painted red. But my apartment feels as big as Union Station.

What are you doing for your birthday? I'd tell you what I am not going to do on your birthday, but I'm sure you've not forgotten that was to be my wedding day.

I see your father everywhere—that jaunty smile and his knack for sweet-talking even shaggy old four-legged goats into a new pair of pumps. Such flair he had. I don't know—if I saw your face at this moment, I'd drown in tears, the way you resemble him.

Without your father's tutelage . . . well, suffice it to say, I owe him everything. What a one-of-a-kind human being. I miss him with all my heart, as I am sure you do.

My mother and sister promise and repromise a visit, but it's just window dressing, a tactic to cut our conversations short. Not that I'm opposed to stylish window displays, mind you, but only if they're <u>sincere</u>!

Could you consider a visit to Kansas City? Please? Pretty please?

I'd get you a birthday present and you'd get to see all the hard work I've done on the Bootery. Why, everyone, no matter how bereaved, cannot help but be buoyed by a new pair of shoes. I have a pair, just arrived, with your name on them. They're not gaudy. Nothing I'd wear. But I perceive your quiet style better than you think I do.

Dinner out. A new pair (or two) of fall shoes. The big city. ME!!!

Say you'll come. I promise I'll not snivel and sniff.

Most sincerely,
Celeste Simmons, Proprietor

P.S. Thank you again for the store.
P.P.S. I've finally mastered the cash register.
P.P.S. $ $ $ Ching-ching!!!!!!!!

I lower the letter to my lap, shake my head.

Celeste.

Her letter was terrible and also okay—even the tiniest bit sincere, in a Celeste kind of way. My face feels brushed by a magician's wand.

I smile.

Birds chatter on our telephone line. I wonder how our spindly phone pole can support all that gossip. I picture Celeste chattering to her customers, projecting herself, trying so hard to make that store a home.

Why wouldn't I go visit her? I can't help it if my feet are over-dressed. It's my fate!

I slap the letter off my palm, thinking for the second time today that the more you belong with people, the more there is to do.

CHAPTER 27

"*Julia?*" Olive squawks through the phone loudly enough for all three of us to hear.

"Why, yes, Olive . . . ," Mrs. Nesbitt replies.

"Tell Avery that my two big *pains*—you know, in my quadrant? They disappeared in the night."

Dr. Nesbitt looks up from his oatmeal, grins.

"I have a thank-you for him, if you and Iris could stop by for it right away."

"Of course. We'll come this morning after we take Avery to work."

Mrs. Nesbitt hangs up and claps. "Ha! Pansy and Dot made off."

We raise our coffee cups.

Mrs. Nesbitt's eyes darken. "But the worst is yet to come: Olive's thank-you gift. Find the Digestive Support Powder, Iris. We are going to need a dose."

"What does Olive mean by a 'thank-you'?" I ask Mrs. Nesbitt in the car. "Thank you for what? Is it telephone code-talk for something else?"

Mrs. Nesbitt gives me a wary look. I keep my eye on the rearview mirror, imagining Cecil on our tail. By the time we reach Olive's my stomach and her hankie are in knots.

But no stomach elixir could curb the bitter mix of ingredients Olive delivers when we arrive. A note for us from Pansy.

Cecil is crazy
he will come lookin for Dot
never ever let him in
don't turn your back either

Olive stares straight ahead without blinking. Mrs. Nesbitt is absolutely pale. My hands tingle. Should I eat the evidence like Dot did? It's already boring a hole in my stomach.

Olive squares her shoulders, pours us coffee that smells like burnt mud, and marches to the renter's wall with a tumbler. She puts the glass to the wallpaper and her ear to the glass. Her eyes shift. She frowns, motions to me. "Iris, come here. Fine-tune your ears."

I hold my breath and listen with full concentration.

Mrs. Nesbitt keeps a champion poker face, which is a tremendous support, but I am desperate to know if I am, or am not, supposed to hear something invisible.

"You see?" Olive says with a smug expression that means we both have solved the mystery. "Just as I suspected."

"I . . . uh . . ." I pretend to prick my ears. Knit my forehead.

Olive nods. "They took that water-maker."

"Who?" Mrs. Nesbitt says.

"Pansy and Dot."

"Took the *dog*?" I ask.

Olive rubs her palms together. "Yep!"

Mrs. Nesbitt chimes in. "Why, that must surely be a relief, Olive. Three pains gone."

"That leaves the fourth: Cecil. That stinkard isn't fit to sit at the Devil's dinner table."

I nod solemnly, determined not to say another word.

Olive stares down her spectacles. "I ask you: Who would be a worse dining companion than Lucifer?"

We sit speechless. Mrs. Nesbitt shoots me a look, then we both say together: "Cecil!"

Olive shakes a finger. "The stories Pansy's sister told me about him. That polecat . . . hellhound."

"Savage," Mrs. Nesbitt adds.

But underneath we know that no amount of name-calling can stop Pansy's prediction.

"He knows I was acquainted with Pansy's sister. He's already on the prowl. Drove by earlier this morning and again just now."

"What?" I walk to the window. "How could you see through the curtain?"

Olive says smugly, "I know the timbre of his automobile engine."

We stand to leave. Olive shoves a jar the color of pond scum in my hand. "Okra," she says. "Stewed. For Avery."

Hawks circle above, their high-pitched cries echoing off the high bluffs behind the house. We drive off, the okra sloshing between us, slimy as slugs. Mrs. Nesbitt grips Henry. I grip the wheel, check the mirror a dozen times down the narrow bluff road from Olive's. Against our better judgment, we go the long way, by Cecil's.

The volcano looks dormant. There is not the usual laundry on the line, just the ratty outhouse door hung open and his lopsided farm cart. The car is gone. I imagine him scouring the rutted back roads of Wellsford, a bottle in one hand, his head hung out the car window, sniffing for Dot.

I shudder, adjust the throttle, and steer us home.

My eyes don't look the way I want.

I stare into the buffet mirror and then try to draw them onto stationery. But they aren't even. They look like they belong to two different people. Daddy's right. I am no artist. I've just chewed a perfectly good pencil and wasted paper. At least it has taken my mind off Cecil for a few hours.

I need help that I can't possibly ask for. I can't tell Mrs. Nesbitt I want to send Leroy a picture of my eyes. Just that. My eyes. It would sound stupid.

And Dr. Nesbitt—he has elegant handwriting, but I could never explain my plan to him. It's too personal, too private and . . . romantic. He'd be mortified. That side of him seems locked up tight. He must have had his heart broken long ago, or he loves somebody who is married, or . . . I don't know.

What I do know from Mrs. Nesbitt, the one time I barely hinted at the subject, is that he is a confirmed bachelor.

Oh, Dr. Nesbitt, could you help me? Leroy sent me his hands and I want to send him a drawing of my eyes he can look into . . . Oh, God. Forget that.

But Mrs. Nesbitt, standing in my bedroom doorway, comes right out and asks, "What are you drawing, Iris? Can I see?"

My mouth feels full of ashes. "My eyes," I croak. "I'm just practicing my eyes." I hand her a pile of rejects.

She shuffles through the pictures, smiles. "You have beautiful golden eyes, Iris. Your heart is in them, and there's intelligence and humor and ache. I understand why you can't capture it all."

"I want to send them to Leroy," I say. Tears well up, the way they always do when I say outright what I want. "I can't ask anyone to draw them, it's so . . ."

Mrs. Nesbitt gets that far-off, crossword-solving expression. "I see."

Later at supper, after Dr. Nesbitt has announced he will work out of home for a few days in case Cecil "comes to call," Mrs. Nesbitt clears her throat and says, "Avery, Iris has in mind to have a drawing of her eyes done."

A swallow of ham stops dead in my throat. Dr. Nesbitt blinks at me, then nods. Amazingly he does not ask why I want such a thing.

"Is that something maybe Marsden could do for her?" she asks softly.

Dr. Nesbitt stops his napkin in midair. I feel the air tighten around us. He and Mrs. Nesbitt exchange a look that speaks deeply about something—a subject far beyond Leroy and me.

Dr. Nesbitt drags his spoon back and forth through a sauce dish of okra. "When do you need this, Iris?"

Mrs. Nesbitt gives me an encouraging "just go ahead and tell him" look. "It's . . . uh, for Leroy. It's not a rush. Just . . . well, when I tried to draw them myself using the mirror, they turned out awful."

He lays both palms faceup on the table, then turns them over. His eyes are shadows. He sniffs and walks his plate to the sink. With his back to me he asks, "Do you have a photograph of yourself, a picture that captures . . ."

"Not a recent one. I'd need to have one taken."

"That's easy enough," Mrs. Nesbitt says. "We can do that in town tomorrow."

The curve of Dr. Nesbitt's back, his hands gripping

the sink, and the tilt of his head are like his mother's in the oil painting above the piano. He looks to be at a crossroads—stuck by the seriousness of what to do or say.

I remember how I used to worry that the air between Daddy and me wasn't strong enough to hold us together. But this room is thick with feeling and mystery. The subject we're speaking about is my eyes, but the focus is really something else, something I don't understand.

"I think I know the kind of expression you want, Iris. I have an artist friend in New York . . . Marsden." Dr. Nesbitt's voice is husky, almost a whisper. "The man who painted Mother can draw your eyes. We just need to send a photograph."

"Thank you," I say quietly. I recall the picture of the artist I saw on Dr. Nesbitt's desk.

We do the dishes in silence. Dr. Nesbitt rinses one plate for almost a minute, leaves soap smears on another. But I just take whatever he hands me and dry it. Mrs. Nesbitt watches him while sipping her tea. The warm glow in her eyes seems to cast a halo around her son.

CHAPTER 28

Five long rings rattle me awake.

Emergency call!

I shoot out of bed, step right on Marie.

Pansy! Cecil!

Something horrible.

I hear Dr. Nesbitt race out of his bedroom to the phone. I light my lamp, carry it to Mrs. Nesbitt's room, and help her out of bed. We stand together in the kitchen, blinking, conjuring the worst.

Dr. Nesbitt's pale gray nightshirt waves ghosty around his ankles. His bare toes are long and bent. I look away, hope he hasn't seen me staring. Mrs. Nesbitt's hair is a silver tangle down her back. My robe is inside out. Only Marie looks her normal self. We, and surely everybody else on our party line, await the operator's voice with news guaranteed to be bad.

Dr. Nesbitt's shoulders slump with the report. He turns to us, disbelief and sadness in his voice. "It's . . . it's Newt Futter. Hung himself in his barn."

Mrs. Nesbitt's eyes narrow. Her mouth looks to be chewing something not fit to swallow.

Dr. Nesbitt hooks the receiver and says to the floor, "I have to pronounce him dead."

We stare at the phone, as though it is at fault somehow.

"The sheriff's coming to pick me up on his way over." Dr. Nesbitt stops, raps his knuckles on the table. "Newt Futter was a nice man. Had two boys."

Within the time it takes him to put on clothes, the county car arrives. Its headlamps bleach the side of our shed. With his black bag and a look of grim determination, Dr. Nesbitt hurries out, leaving us to balance the weight of it all.

I didn't know Mr. Futter, but I can imagine the scene at his barn—the bewildered gathering of friends and neighbors, the sleepy boys huddled in the house.

Mrs. Nesbitt turns to me. "This isn't the first hanging for Avery. Three years ago, for some ungodly reason, the authorities waited for him to arrive to cut a poor fellow down. It's one of the few times I have seen him mad." She sighs. "People will count on him tonight because he's seen it before. There's strange comfort in that."

We lean down and rub Marie between the ears, then I

let her out to patrol the chicken house. With hot tea and the crossword, we attempt to fill the deep well Mr. Futter's decision has dug inside us.

"Noctambulation," Mrs. Nesbitt says. "Twelve letters."

"Is that a word? Noc—oh, I see, night plus ambulation. Walk at night . . . nightwalker."

"That's only eleven. It's 'sleepwalking.'"

"Good." I look at the puzzle. "Diabolical. Five letters . . . starts with 'c.'"

Mrs. Nesbitt spells on her crooked fingers. "C–r–u–e–l."

We fill several columns and have a second cup of tea. Well past three we still wait for Dr. Nesbitt. The moon joins our vigil, full and absolutely brilliant.

Car lights snake up the drive, sweep the shed, and flash oddly over the back porch. "Avery. Finally." Mrs. Nesbitt's voice is weary and relieved.

I step to the porch. The car, partway on the yard, illuminates the clothesline and my sawhorse full of shotgun targets. The taillights wash the chicken coop red.

I squint into the headlamps. The engine sputters and chugs. The tailpipe sparks. In one horrid moment I realize it's not Dr. Nesbitt . . . or the sheriff.

My stomach drops. "It's Cecil," I hiss through the screen.

He's not wearing his greasy straw hat. He tilts his head back. In one swig he empties a moonshine bottle and hurls it out the window. It bounces once and shatters against the clothesline pole. The car door squawks open; Cecil turns, peers out.

Mrs. Nesbitt steps right next to me on the porch and

passes the flashlight to me. I aim the beam in Cecil's face.

He squints up at us, swipes his mouth. A pulse pounds in my neck.

Mrs. Nesbitt asks, "It's the middle of the night, Cecil. What's the matter?"

"What'd you do with Dot?" he snarls. "She belongs to me." Oily automobile exhaust fills our yard and our noses, chokes the crickets into silence.

"Dot?" Mrs. Nesbitt sounds as though she has not thought of her in months. "What do you mean?"

Cecil swings a leg out. His foot gropes for ground. "You helped her run off."

"We did not!" Mrs. Nesbitt says with force and finality.

Cecil stands and steadies himself against the car door. "Or she's hiding . . ." His gaze shifts from us to the kitchen door to our storm-cellar doors. He takes a few steps, holding a hand behind his back, stopping not more than ten yards from the porch step. "DOT!" he demands. "Get out here!"

Mrs. Nesbitt and I stand silent. I see moonlight flash off his bald head and the hunting knife in his hand. He takes another step toward the porch.

Pansy's warning circles through my head: Never let him in, don't turn your back . . .

"She's too smart to hide here—so close to home," Mrs. Nesbitt says matter-of-factly. "Have you contacted the authorities?"

"Unless . . . ," I say slowly, turning to Mrs. Nesbitt, "would she hide in our shed?"

"No!" Mrs. Nesbitt says—her tone incredulous.

I ever so slightly nudge her elbow, hand her the flashlight. She pauses a moment, points at the garage. "You don't mean in *there*?" Cecil follows her gaze, stumbles in that direction. I step backward into the kitchen, grab the shotgun, and slide it beside me.

The double barrel feels powerful, deadly in my fist.

Out of the corner of my eye I see Marie streak across the chicken yard onto the lawn. In a split second she lunges at Cecil like she has eaten a stick of dynamite.

"Marie. NO!" I scream.

She charges and clamps her teeth in Cecil's calf. He jerks back, cursing and kicking. She hits the ground hard.

Fury rises in me. In one burst I hoist the gun to my shoulder, cock the hammer, aim high, and pull the trigger. The recoil knocks me against the doorframe. Gunpowder sears my nose. Mrs. Nesbitt grabs my raised arm to balance herself.

Cecil looks skyward as though the shot spray was a swarm of mosquitoes.

"MARIE!" Mrs. Nesbitt says her eyes fixed on Cecil. "Come here."

She doesn't. She springs to her feet and leaps back, snarling at him. He walks slowly forward, waving the blade, grinning. "Come on, girl. I got ya . . ."

Cecil throws the knife down and in one horrendous sweep grabs Marie around the neck with both hands. He stands and holds her out to us, writhing and twisting.

I cock the second hammer.

"Shoot again, I strangle the mutt," he says. His voice is thick, taunting.

I lower the gun, stopped cold by Marie's cries, her pathetic whimper.

Then he wheels around and throws her into the car. "Can't call the sheriff, can ya. He's busy tonight. So's the doc. I know who you're in cahoots with. Dot won't get far."

Cecil gets in, slams the car door, and yanks the wheel. He careens down the drive, bumping our telephone pole, then fishtails away, scraping the mailbox as he turns—not left toward home, but right toward Olive's, leaving the stink of hate, exhaust, and gunpowder in his wake.

My mind flashes on Marie limp on the car seat and Olive at home asleep. I run into the kitchen for the phone. It's dead. I burst outside, furious at that bully forcing his sick, drunk self on everybody.

I swipe tears from my cheeks. "I've gotta go warn Olive."

But Mrs. Nesbitt plants Henry right in front of me. "Stop." I turn. Her look could split stone. "If you are going, so am I."

And in moments the two of us and a third passenger— the shotgun on Mrs. Nesbitt's lap—head out.

My stomach feels like I've swallowed Cecil's knife. I focus beyond the glow of our headlamps, Mrs. Nesbitt's hand on my knee. I yank at the corner of my robe caught in the car door, clamp my teeth, and drive.

In a moment we see taillights. I speed up a bit, thinking out loud, "For Olive's he'll go straight, left toward the bluff road, then right to her house." The road rumbles under us, the moon a spotlight on this impossible night.

But suddenly Cecil's car lurches left, scales a shallow ditch, and bumps onto a pasture.

I jiggle the steering wheel. "What's he doing?"

"Either it's a shortcut or a trap," Mrs. Nesbitt warns. "Don't follow him."

The trail of matted grass behind his headlamps looks like a lit fuse. A covey of quail swoops up—hundreds of noisy birds reflecting the moon. Night creatures skitter in front of our tires. I ignore them.

"Now left," Mrs. Nesbitt directs at the intersection. We make a sharp turn onto the road that intersects Olive's. Through the hedgerow, I see Cecil zigzag across the grassy field beside us. He guns his engine, bucking every which way. The pasture is slow going. I force a pitiful image of Marie from my mind.

We reach the bluff road before he does. I brake, start to make the right turn to Olive's, then stop short. Cecil's car has burst out of the stubble onto the narrow gravel stretch, but instead of turning toward us, it jerks wildly left, spins once around, slides sideways and is gone.

I blink at the instant emptiness. Absorb the moment of silence before the earth receives the blow.

Plumes of dirt soar skyward. Flames tower. Sparks shoot the moon. We watch the sky turn from black to gold. Brambles and trees look hit by lightning.

Hot wind and grit tick off the windshield. I swallow smoke. Mrs. Nesbitt coughs into her sleeve.

I sit numb, as though Cecil's death car has plowed right through me.

The flames shrink. From the bluff, small explosions punctuate the night. We stare at the dirty orange sky, then bow our heads, rub each other's hands. Softly Mrs. Nesbitt says, "The volcano finally erupted. The devil took our angel."

CHAPTER 29

I sit on Olive's front stoop and gaze down the bluff road. The moon has faded, exhausted like the rest of us. My throat is raw, my chest choked with smoke and a sadness I can't cough away. *Stop that,* Daddy used to say when I was little, because coughing reminded him of Mama. I wonder if he'd scold me now.

In the distance the wreck still steams, pink in the dawn light. The sheriff is down there now and Dr. Nesbitt and some other folks. But not me.

Olive has given me a glass of water, a damp washrag, and a pillow to sit on. She and Mrs. Nesbitt are resting inside. Except for the long telephone conversation I had summoning Dr. Nesbitt and the sheriff from the Futters, I have hardly spoken since we arrived here. I can't even think. I don't want to.

I hear men's voices and car doors slamming. The county car snakes this way. I cover my face. It means there will have to be talk—descriptions, explanations, plans. Tears run under my fingers, in my mouth, down my neck. My hankie is soaked. I tilt my head and blot my face against the collar of my robe.

Mrs. Nesbitt and Olive come to the door when Dr. Nesbitt and the sheriff get out of the car. I look up, desperate to see Marie with them.

She is not.

Dr. Nesbitt hugs his mother a long while, then the older ladies go inside. He sits beside me on the step. His eyes are rimmed red, his shirt dirty and stuck to his back. He smoothes away a soggy curl matted to my cheek and looks at me with such concern and respect that I straighten my shoulders a bit and raise my chin.

We go inside to Olive's round breakfast table. The sheriff rubs his forehead, as though enough massage will revive his frayed mind. His fingernails are grimy, his cuffs stained dark. Olive brings a pitcher of lemonade that is surprisingly sweet and cold. I pour it carefully, the same amount in each glass.

The sheriff clears his throat, begins slowly. "Cecil was thrown from the car before it exploded."

My heart skips. Mrs. Nesbitt looks stricken.

"He did *not* survive, if that concerns you. But we were

able to make certain assumptions based on evidence."

I watch a sunbeam spread across Olive's dingy carpet. I want it to crawl into my lap.

"The car trunk was full of liquor bottles—thus the series of smaller explosions you described over the telephone. But Mr. Deets's fatal driving maneuvers were a result of more than moonshine. The deceased, in addition to the predictable injuries, was covered with bite marks on his arms and hands, even his neck."

"Marie," I whisper.

Dr. Nesbitt shakes his head. "She was a hobo dog at heart, no stranger to the rougher side."

The sheriff slides paperwork in front of him. "I'm sorry, Avery, but I need the certificate, if you could . . ."

Dr. Nesbitt fills in the form: Missouri Bureau of Vital Statistics Standard Certificate of Death. His handwriting is calming to watch. He fills in the date—Sept 24, 1926—then turns to the sheriff. "Lowell, I don't know this information— the name of Cecil's father, his mother's birthplace."

I look off. Never once have I considered his having parents. What must they have been like? How do you raise a Cecil?

"Why, I just imagined he crawled out of a flaming hole in the ground," Olive says, draining her lemonade. "And tonight, thank God, he crawled back into the inferno."

We shift in our chairs. Dr. Nesbitt clears his throat, swallows, and proceeds to the "Medical Particulars" section. On the line that begins "I hereby certify," he prints:

Cecil Deets—deceased.

"Deader 'n hell," the sheriff remarks with a sigh.

"Beautifully put," Olive says as the officer folds the form into his pocket. After he leaves she remarks, "Cecil could put two and two together. He'd been stalking all of us since Dot left. He knew that when the Sheriff and Avery were at Newt's, he could come hunting her."

Olive wipes her mouth with a gray hankie. "Demonic doesn't mean dumb." She looks from Dr. Nesbitt to his mother to me and proceeds cautiously with her next remark. "And *dead* doesn't always mean *gone*."

"Oh no, Olive!" I say. "Cecil is *gone*."

"But the dog . . . ," Olive says, "is *invisible* now. Not gone."

Mrs. Nesbitt sighs, her voice weary. "Forgive me, Olive, but I can't hear about your dog problems right now."

"I am not speaking of *my* dog difficulties. I am telling you that Marie is not gone unless you make her so." There is fierceness and kindness in Olive's face. "Dead and gone versus a spirit—there is a difference. It's a choice we make with loved ones who've passed."

Olive looks toward the door and smiles slightly, as though she has seen Marie trot through it.

I climb from our car and walk across the yard determined to avoid the broken liquor bottle, the ruts and tracks, the flashlight left on the porch. But of course I do look at them and, hardest of all, the moment I step in my room I stare at Marie's lumpy blue blanket on the floor.

My mind flashes to Atchison, to Daddy's slippers—how they also held his shape.

My sheets and pillow are a rumpled mess. I grab Rosie and sit on the rug by Marie's bed. There's dog hair and the curve of her back pressed in it. I fill my nose with her scent.

Everything is so still, so unbearably quiet and empty. My stomach knots around the raw pain of missing her. I think of her stumpy tail, her habit of getting stepped on, her fierce love and protection of us.

"Marie?" I whisper. "Are you all right?"

I sit a while, watch my goddesses watching me. I smell coffee brewing, hear the telephone ring for the third time since we've been home.

I run my finger around the blanket's bound edge. "I love you."

My back aches. I stand and stretch, not knowing what to do with myself. By the wall a tiny movement catches my eye. I bend down. A furry, silver-brown spider is building her web between my bedpost and the window. It's in an odd spot and the design isn't perfect. The tiny silk ropes are crooked. It is more a loopy oval than a circle, but the spider just keeps spinning back and forth as naturally as can be, knitting her new home in the air.

CHAPTER 30

I wake up mad.

Rage at Cecil—that walking, talking accident of a human—mixes with other rough feelings, especially the ones about Daddy.

I could pull that trigger a thousand times more. I grip my pillow and sob.

I don't try to make myself stop crying anymore, Daddy. That rule of yours was stupid.

People don't have all the time in the world either.

You were wrong about that, too.

You were wrong about lots of things: Iris, you can't draw. . . .

You should project yourself more. . . . Shoes make the woman. . . .

You were wrong to say "I love you" and not mean it.

It wasn't fair of you to make me hold my coughs. No little girl should have to stifle a cough!

"I am going to let what's true inside me out, or I'll end up like you, a suede salesman with no insides at all!" I yell. I march outside to the bench, ragged feelings crashing in me.

Oak-branch reflections slice like black cracks across the sunny birdbath water. I cry hard, my fists in my lap. I can't stand that Marie isn't here.

I rock and hug myself for the longest time.

I know I have lots of dusting to do in my cellar of ghosts. But I have a plan now. If even one more ghost dares to show up, I'll do exactly what Pansy said: *Never ever let him in.*

September 30, 1926

Dear Miss Baldwin,

It has been my challenge and pleasure to capture the essence of your eyes on paper. I used the recent photograph as a guide and shaded them with the intelligence and grace Julia and Avery find in you.

I pause, lower the note to my lap. My cheeks burn. What on earth have the Nesbitts said?

The young man about to receive them should be warned of their potency—but then, if he has looked into your eyes once, he already knows. It's a wonder he can do much else!

Please find the drawing enclosed. When you gaze into it I do so hope you see longing and strength and passion looking back.

We will meet when I visit Wellsford this winter. I do so miss my teasing with Julia—the last goddess left on earth—and, of course, her son—my inspiration.

Life paints each of us with a different stroke.

Warmly,
Marsden White

I reread the letter, study the last line—a perfect vine of black ink across the page.

I slide the sketch paper from the envelope. It is thick stock and only as big as my hand. The tissue falls away. I take a breath and look into my eyes.

Someone whole and loved looks back.

I tilt my head to absorb the drawing. My eyes look lit from the inside, glowing.

I blink once, twice—just the way I used to with Mama. And somewhere inside me, Mama blinks back.

"I am whole and loved," I tell her. "*We* are whole . . . and loved."

In the parlor I study the portrait of Mrs. Nesbitt that Marsden painted after her son died. You cannot see her eyes. They are lost in shadow. She has told me, "I could not look at myself then. I was too weak and empty, too unbearably sad."

I think how brave she was to have it painted with all her pain showing. How she must have trusted him. His signature, a rosy sweep in the corner, is confident and strong. Maybe their time together was just right. He painted her sadness without telling her what to feel or do about it, without any answers or advice.

In my room I smooth my coverlet and place the drawing in the middle of my bed. I arrange Leroy's hands on either side. I gather my hair and lift it, let it fall a bit at a time against my back, study the picture arrangement.

It isn't right.

I move the drawings. Put my eyes at the top, then below.

No.

"They don't go together yet—too many bits and pieces," I tell the bedspread.

I get my stationery and pen. I know what's missing.

September 30, 1926
Dear Leroy,

Come for my birthday or sooner. Go with us to visit Kansas City.
The drawings of your hands are everything but warm enough.

Iris

P.S. I have a present for you. . . .

Dr. Nesbitt puts my letter to Leroy in his breast pocket, then steps around the shotgun and out to his car. He is going by the post office for me and then to work.

Although I hear Cecil's death car a hundred times a day, the real threat of him is over. The Nesbitts and Olive and I have talked and talked about the events of that night— Marie, our teamwork, the what-ifs. It's good to do. Helps calm our nerves. Helps us move on.

Dr. Nesbitt has already advertised for a new tenant to rent our land, but none of us knows what to do with Cecil's haunted monument of a house less than a mile away.

"We can't tear it down yet, even though it's on our property," Dr. Nesbitt says at the table later that evening. Olive is over for supper.

"Why not?" Mrs. Nesbitt says, with an air of not being bullied by anything Deets.

"Technically Pansy and Dot are the next of kin and they have the right to what's in it," he says.

"Only rats and rot," Olive remarks after a stiff sip of brandy. Her eyes narrow. "Who says they need to know of Cecil's passing? Why would they care?"

"But Olive . . ."

Olive sits like she's holding court and takes a deep breath. "Lest you forget, I alone know the accurate address of the sister, and I alone may or may not correctly offer it to the authorities when their first attempt at notification comes back in the returned mail as surely it will." Olive swipes her mouth. "And we all know that the sister may very well not know where Pansy and Dot are anyway. In fact, I sincerely hope she does not."

"Because . . . ?" Dr. Nesbitt asks.

"Because a hundred years from now would still be a hair too soon to see those two again. Don't get me wrong. I am glad we did it. But enough mayhem and tongue-swallowing terror!" She fans her nose. "They can live without a collection of Cecil's crusty, frayed undergarments." Olive demonstrates her disdain for

Cecil's undershorts by dropping her napkin.

Mrs. Nesbitt lowers her fork and looks toward the ceiling.

Olive charges on. "His hemorrhoids, his rusted pots and pans, his rodent infested flour and sugar sacks, his . . ."

"Amen," Dr. Nesbitt says.

Olive raps her index finger on the table. "He was nothing but a poisonous serpent, slithering where he shouldn't."

"Amen again!" Dr. Nesbitt says, with a note of *okay, that's enough*.

"Ah . . . yes." Olive softens and dabs her eyes with her favorite hankie, the one she refers to as Old Dainty.

After Dr. Nesbitt drives Olive home, he jokes as he comes in the kitchen, "It is amazing how Olive can ruin a meal even without cooking it."

I lie in bed, trying hard to think of something besides Leroy's hands. I am dying for him to get here and then go with us to Kansas City to see Celeste's store and celebrate my birthday. So much life has poured in and out of me this year, I can barely remember my old self. As Mrs. Nesbitt put it, "A hundred new Irises have bloomed this summer!"

Three early birthday presents from the Nesbitts are on my dresser: applications for college. "Seeds," Mrs. Nesbitt called them. "Someday," she added when she saw the stricken look on my face. "*Someday* you will go on to school, Iris."

But I could only stutter, and she knew why. Because "someday" sounded like "after I die."

"Don't worry. I'll not abandon Henry. He's not ready to retire," she said. "But this is a *farm*, after all. So I can plant all the seeds I want!"

But before anything else, before I turn sixteen or go to college or even feed the chickens, I have two things to finish. The first is the compartment in Mama's secretary I've been avoiding. What's in there will rouse Daddy's ghost.

CHAPTER 31

It's early. I raise the parlor shades and sit at Mama's desk wrapped in my old chenille robe. Something inside rattles like a box full of pulled teeth when I slide the compartment open. I fish out a lumpy envelope with a scrap of brittle newspaper clipped to the outside: Mama's obituary.

> Anna Jane Kohler Baldwin
> aged 31, died Monday at
> Holcomb Sanatorium. She is
> survived by her husband
> Charles Winn Baldwin and

a daughter. Funeral arrangements
courtesy of Lundgrun
Funeral Parlor, Atchison.

Just like Daddy—all business. I turn the clipping over.
He reduced Mama's life story to something smaller than
the foot powder advertisement on the back. Nothing
about *her*, or her parents, or where she was born. Does
Anna Baldwin's daughter have a name, Daddy, or did
you forget that too? I'm surprised you didn't mention
the store: *Anna's husband is the proprietor of the popular Baldwin
Shoes.*

Mrs. Nesbitt sits above me in her portrait—achingly
beautiful, heartbreakingly real. That's what I want, an
oil painting of Mama by someone who knew her, loved
her. Not stiff and posed, but shimmering with her feelings.

I recall Dr. Nesbitt's comments about Mama's sanatorium when I'd finally gathered the nerve to ask him about
it. He'd been there years ago, before it closed. He said that
"brave" is not enough of a word to describe living for years
like Mama did, never knowing if your next trip would be
back home or to heaven.

I open the envelope expecting to find her death certificate and some of my baby teeth, but instead there's a
photograph, rhinestone buttons, and a letter I have never
seen, dated a month before Mama died.

October 20, 1916

Dearest Iris,

This is not my handwriting. A lovely nurse named Elizabeth is writing this for me. Do you like the picture? I do. It's my favorite. You look ready to ride that pumpkin around the block!

In the photograph I straddle a fat pumpkin with the stem gripped in both hands. I peer out from under a huge tipsy hair bow—a dollop of satin whipped cream plopped on my head.

Your father has promised to read this letter to you when he gives you my Christmas present. I hope you like it. I had Mrs. Andrews make it out of my blue velvet dress— the one you love, with the rhinestone buttons we call stars.

Do you remember being three years old and counting all twelve stars when you sat on my lap? You will find only eleven in this envelope, because one is sewn inside your present.

Rosie! Mama had Mrs. Andrews make her for me.

I run to my room. Rosie is so full of holes that Mama's star is surely gone, swept into a dustpan and tossed. I sit on my bed and knead every lump and hollow.

I shut my eyes and explore Rosie's paw, finding the one thick place I used to rub over my lip. And there it is—the little rhinestone button, Mama's secret buried deep in stuffing, hidden for ten years right in front of my face.

For a moment it is that first Christmas right after she died. I remember receiving Rosie and naming her. I remember Mrs. Andrews smiling. She must have believed Daddy read Mama's letter to me so I knew the secret. But he never did. I wipe my eyes on Rosie, carry her to the parlor, and read on.

Give your stuffed kitty a name and hug and talk to her whenever you miss me. I hope you like the rose sachets tucked inside.

When you feel the secret button, remember the love we hold inside for each other.

I am shining on you every minute.

With all my love forever,
Mama

I smooth the paper. Breathe in, breathe out. Bolt the cellar door against Daddy—how he could have let this letter be "lost" so long. Tears come again. I arrange the buttons in a semicircle, then a circle—a constellation—with Mama's invisible star in the center. Midnight blue thread is still hooked to some of them. They rattle when I bump the leg of the desk, then settle back in place.

I scoop them up, shake their solid weight in my hand.

I massage Rosie's paw button between my fingers, imagine when she was a dress with all of Mama inside her. In my imaginary portrait, rhinestones appear in a glittering line from Mama's throat to her waist. Each one is highlighted by a perfect dab of white paint.

Leroy opens the envelope, studies my present— Marsden's drawing—and shakes his head. "Damn." He gives me a "what are you trying to do to me" look.

"You *like* it?"

He nods. Looks me in the eye. "*Damn*, Iris." He puts the drawing back in the envelope and slides it into his shirt pocket. "It's . . . amazing. Thank you."

At dusk, under a moonless sky, we sit on a low hill down the road from the Nesbitts' and watch stars poke through the velvet night. It looks like I have tossed my handful of buttons into the sky.

Leroy points up. "The constellations are a compass for birds and sailors and . . ."

"Hobos," I say.

Crickets converse. Trains call each other along the horizon. It's dark now. I use Leroy's faint shaving-cream smell as my compass to find him eight inches away. "Trains don't need to navigate with stars," I say. "They never get lost."

We listen to the breeze loop through the grassy land spread below us. Leroy shifts. "I'm going to give you something for your birthday now."

"A present? Now? How will I see it?"

"You won't. It's something I packaged up."

"Packaged up?"

"Yeah." He turns, takes a deep breath, and strokes his fingertip across my lips. Then he kisses me.

I sit there perfectly hollow, letting the kiss pour in.

"Okay?" he whispers.

"Yes." He kisses me again. "Are there sixteen presents in your package?" I ask. "One for every year?"

"No, one for every star."

A movement, a rhythm happens—our lips together, then apart, so we can come together again. The hill comes loose, spins skyward.

"What about the tarnished stars?" I say.

"Two kisses each."

"And the invisible ones?"

"At least three."

Something flutters past. I grab Leroy's arm and look up. "It's the goddesses spying on us," I say.

Leroy brushes his lips across my ear. "Are they shocked to see us kissing?" he whispers.

"No . . . jealous." I shiver.

Leroy touches my arms. "You cold?"

"I don't know. I'm . . ."

I hear him pulling off his shirt. In a moment he wraps it around me. His heat is still in it. We sit looking straight ahead. I catch my breath, feel the thick envelope against my heart. Can he know that right now he has *all* of me in his pocket?

"Now *you're* cold," I squeak.

"No, Iris. I am definitely not cold." He stretches his legs, crosses his ankles.

I turn to him. I can just see the outline of his face, his bare shoulders and chest. Never have I seen this much of a person, this smooth endless sweep of skin.

"God . . . Leroy . . ." I move behind him. "Don't turn around." His back is . . . what? More manageable? Or . . . at least his back is . . . not his *front*.

I take a huge breath, let it out slowly. *Okay*. I stretch my fingers wide, measure across his shoulders. I trace and retrace the matching ridges and craters on each side. My hands slide partway down his arms and back up. I touch his neck, comb through his hair. "It's tangled."

"The wind."

"You've got goose bumps."

"That's the wind too."

I lay my palms flat on his back. "I can feel your heart pounding clear through."

"Can you hear it?" he asks.

I lay my ear against his skin. "Perfectly."

I find two long scars in the amazingly soft skin on his side. "What's this?"

He shakes his head. "Cuts from the ice truck. They're okay."

Starting between his shoulder blades, I roll my knuckles down the chain of his spine until the arc of it reverses, sinks, and disappears. The sides of my thumbs rub the curved furrows of his ribs.

"Ask me what I'm doing," I whisper.

His voice is low. "What are you doing?"

"Polishing your back."

"Good."

"I'm leaving some dents."

He shifts, stretches. "Good."

His back is the only real thing in the universe, plus kissing and stars and buried secrets and his shoulders and muscles and kissing . . .

I lift his hair, whisper in his ear. "I think I'm lost."

"Good." He turns. "I'll come find you. . . ."

I could not sleep all night, but I don't care one bit. This morning the four of us are on the way to Kansas City. We have already stopped in Atchison so I could see Carl and hear the shoe-store gossip. We have driven past my old house. It looked good—the leaves were raked and there was a pillow in the porch swing.

At my request, Dr. Nesbitt is taking the route past the cemetery. I have one last stop to make before Kansas City.

It is beautiful—clear and cooler than yesterday.

We pass a blur of maple trees caught between the seasons—

with green leaves starting to reveal their crimson secret.

Dr. Nesbitt glances at me in the backseat and stops at the cemetery gate. We peer through the curly wrought iron—upside-down hearts locked together with vines—to the gravestones beyond.

I blink-talk to Mama the way we used to do. *I found our star. I'll meet you down the road*, I say silently to my father.

"Do you want to get out?" Dr. Nesbitt asks.

"No, sir, but I would like to drive now."

Mrs. Nesbitt turns around to me with that penetrating gaze of hers.

While Dr. Nesbitt gets in back beside Leroy, I settle into the driver's seat. Mrs. Nesbitt hands me her glasses to wipe.

"Thank you, dear." She pats my hand, scanning the road ahead.

An anticipation builds. Something—an unspoken *knowing*—moves among us. I see the gritty old image of Daddy and me racing down this very same stretch eight years ago, to that awful crossing.

I feel fear build in me the way it did then—the realization that something was driving Daddy, something I couldn't stop.

In a moment the railroad sign bobs on the horizon.

What?

I press the brake, stop, squint at the sign, certain someone has moved the tracks.

This can't be it . . . so soon. I don't remember it this way.

I grip the steering wheel and now, at this very minute,

I make the connection—how very close Mama's grave is to the crossing.

Was Daddy trying to beat his pain about her that day?

The tracks, thirty feet ahead, are absolutely unremarkable. All is quiet but a lazy fly and the hum of the car engine. I close my eyes and step back through that heavy door in time.

You always had to have the right shoes for your next shiny plan. Or were they for running from sadness, from scars you couldn't polish away, from memories . . . from me?

I wrap myself in my arms and wait for the train to bear down on Daddy and me with its cargo of destruction and deliverance.

But it doesn't.

It's just the four of us, two simple rails, one chipped sign, and a scattering of broken rock.

A fine golden dust dances across our windshield.

Leroy reaches out from the backseat and cups my shoulders in his incredible hands.

I sit a long moment, then turn to Mrs. Nesbitt—so brilliant outside, wrapped in the gold embroidered shawl she wore the first time we met. So wise inside.

I look around at Dr. Nesbitt, knowing he would wait forever until I'm ready to go.

I hold the steering wheel, look both ways, adjust the throttle. No one talks when we bump over the tracks, but I hear them anyway. . . .

Remember, Iris, steer clear of ditches. Use your headlamps. Don't drive in pastures. Aim high. Help hobos and strays. Dust the people you love.

When lost, use the stars.